Acknowledgements

The most important part of any book

I say this because without those who help us there would not be any book written. First, I absolutely love honoring my wife Judy for her patience over the past 40 weeks.

She probably felt as though it was the 40 weeks of Daniel, and somewhere along the way, the Great Tribulation happened!

Sir Vince Dawson, now Knighted the King of artwork did and incredible job on the cover design the overall appearance of the book.

My 'big sister' Billie managed to undangle all of my misplaced participles. Also Ann Taylor's Colorful commentary that inspired me. And I must mention Shirley Middleton and her midnight hours of editing. Perfectionists do make a big difference in this world.

You Can tell that what I just said is true. Just look, I spilled ink on the artwork, messed up the margins and there likely is a mospelled word in here somewhere.

A final thanks to Bishop Kenneth Phillips for his endorsement and all of my other Peers and Pastors who have mentored and befriended me!

Much Love, Louis

The Prodigal Satan

CONTENTS

The Prodigal Satan

 Copies of this publication may be obtained by contacting the author:
theprodigalsatan@gmail.com

The Prodigal Satan

A Jewish Rabbi told a story of a certain man who had two sons. The firstborn was faithful to his Father; the Prodigal was wanton and wasteful. The younger desperately desired to inherit the wealth willed to his elder brother. This led to the breakup of the family and the downfall of the younger son, infamously known as "The Prodigal Son." In the telling of this Parable by Jesus, we are given clues and insight into a story older than time itself!

Jude 1:6 - "You also know that the angels who did not keep their first inheritance but abandoned their own place of home, He has kept in eternal chains in utter darkness, locked up for the judgment of the great Day."

The Prodigal Satan

PROLOGUE ONE

The Prodigal Satan is 'my attempt to use scientific terminology, dressing it up in the liturgical clothing of a cosmic drama.' None of us can answer all the questions all the time, but hopefully this treatise will evolve into a novel so true as to debunk fiction. I present to you, book one, with two to follow.

Prayerfully there will be trilogy, one story past, another present and lastly futuristic. Section one of this novel begins with *'Plot Coupons'* (MacGuffins[1]) from the distant past. These coupons are clues to the cause behind the chaos that was and continues until the present in our universe. Book two will be stylistically written as a novel. Special thanks for book three will be given to Saint John for His time spent on Patmos penning his revelatory prophesy!

World War 1 era actress Pearl White used the term MacGuffin to identify whatever physical object impelled the heroes and villains to pursue each other through the convoluted plots. *'This book is about heroes and villains, Angels and Demons and it clearly contains a complicated plot.'* Filmmaker George Lucas said, a plot coupon should be powerful and the audience should care about it almost as much as the dueling heroes and villains on-screen. So take your time, consider the concepts contained in these coupons. Their clues will come alive as the plot progresses!

1 MacGuffin - A Word describing theatrical clues that may not have significant meaning until the plot unfolds.

The Prodigal Satan

PLOT COUPON ONE
THE BEGINNING OF THE END

What was God doing before He created The Universe? Augustine answered, "since time did not exist, God did not have time to do anything!"

Genesis 1:1-2 - "In the beginning, God created the heavens and the earth. And the Earth, became (not was created) without form and void."

2 Peter 3:5-6 - "For they deliberately suppress this fact, that by the word of God heavens existed long ago and an earth was formed out of water and by means of water. Through these things the world existing at that time was destroyed when it was deluged with water."

There was no void, emptiness, shape, form or embodiment. A nameless, unexplainable entity was all that existed or ever had been. 'It' was everything. 'It' was everywhere. 'It'[1] had no name for there was none other for 'It' to speak to or commune with; although we are told in the Holy Writings the 'It' did counsel with 'Itself.'[2] Thus there was no need for language or sound. Only the quiet stillness of a oneness that none of we earthlings can comprehend existed. In our ongoing quest to define the indefinable using our language, we have assigned the title

"God" to this ineffable one and will refer to 'It' as "Elyon" or ♍[3] from hereon. If you ever care to feel frustrated,

1 "IT" - God before creation.
2 Ephesians 1:11 - "...Who works out all things according to the counsel of His own will."
3 When referring to the unknown gender of Elyon in creation. We will replace he, his or she, hers with the "Divine ME"! ♍ chooses to represents ♍self as the Lamb(Bene Elyon) - Son of God in His Redemptive works. The Ram like symbol ♈ represents Bene Elyon.

try choosing any ending number to count backwards from until you arrive at a number. The futility is that you do not know the origin of the beginning numeral or much less where to start an end or end a start. Yet again in our inane way of doing things we have come to think of and designate such a collection of numbers as "time."

How ironic that if we read backwards our word "time" would become the word *'Emit.'*[1] According to Merriam Webster's dictionary, the word Emit is defined as, "to give out light", or "give utterance," so Emit is where we will start our saga of the beginning. The beginning of *'what'* is the question? Emit was not the beginning of time. There was yet no days, nights, years or seasons. Just Em-it! The EM of IT. Possibly the hint that gave Einstein his theory pertaining to energy and mass. E=MC2. Energy, mass = going at the speed of light, but not by 2 squared, just by 1 supreme. One did it. It did it!

Language becomes extremely difficult here because words like time, when, eventually, occasionally, era, age; none of them apply to the immeasurable Emit. I may use one of these nonexistent words occasionally, simply because I am out of words that did not exist in Emit. So I cannot tell you when Emit began, it is inexplicably "The Beginning." *'There were no calendars, written history, sundials or clocks. Only light and utterance carrying out the creative commands of Elyon in the vastness of eternity!'* The only two clues we have about Elyon is that light is the essence of *'Its'* Being and utterance is the method by which *'It'* announces, allocates and administers power for the making of matter.

We also believe that Elyon is omnipresent. "How is this possible and where is everywhere?" "Wherever anything is," provides us the best definition of "everywhere." If you claimed to arrive at *'nothing'* you would negate *'nothing'* because you

1 EMIT is actions taken before time began.

are matter; matter is *'something'* and you are present.

Famed scientist Einstein proposed that light and time bend in space forming a never ending arch in the vastness of space, which could eventually return to its point of origin. The warping of space creates endless groupings of concentric cosmic circles that equal infinity or better defined as, *'Elyon's everywhere!'*

The Prodigal Satan

PLOT COUPON TWO
AN EXPLOSION CALLED LOGOS

John 1:1 - "In the beginning was the Logos (WORD) and the Logos was with God."

We give credit to the ancient Greeks for defining the intellect and thought processes of the Being to whom we ascribe omniscience as the all-knowing *'Logos.'*[1]

Translated in scripture as *'Word.'*[2] One should specifically acknowledge Anaxagoras who introduced the cosmological concept of Nous (mind), as an ordering force.

A pressing question will be considered here. If indeed omniscience exists, can an *'all knowing'* refuse to know? One of the great biblical theologians wrote, "At one time Elyon *'winked'* at ignorance."[3] It should be noted, *'To know is not to cause.'* Foreknowledge plays no part in, *"Post hoc ergo propter hoc."*[4]

One of the great mysteries that gives us insight into what Elyon desired to happen by *'Emit'* is that ♍ would create something other than ♍-self to be in relationship with.

Did ♍ know, or did ♍ cause the chaotic consequences of a *'free will creation?'* The answer may lie in something as simple as, *'Almost every great romance begins with a wink.'* It appears that Emit was just that; a *'Celestial Courtship'* between Creator, creature and cosmos! Maybe, just maybe there is truth in the old adage, *"Love is Blind."*

1 Logos is a Greek word expressing thought, idea or concept. John 1:14 - "The logos became flesh (Yeshua) and dwelt among us."

2 John 1:1 - "In the beginning was the Word." (Logos)

3 Acts 17:30 - "And the times of this ignorance God winked at, but now commands all men every where to repent:"

4 Latin for "after this, therefore because of this." 'Cause and effect.'

The Prodigal Satan

On command, *'The Infinite Light'* compressed *'It-self'* until *'The Cosmic Everything'* compacted into a minuscule *'creation molecule. It collapsed as its circumference became a subatomic center.'* The creation molecule was the seed of conception. The cogitations[1] of *'The Logos went into labor, contracting with birth-pains of creation.'*

As I attempt to make this plausible, I propose that you consider electrons. They are composed of quarks, which are quite smaller than electrons, made up of muons, gloums, leptoms, femioms, tracheons among others. The power of an omnipotent God is exhibited in these elements. *'Everywhere'* became so concentrated that the unfettered energy of the Godhead erupted in an unimaginable birthing of everything the Logos expressed and expected.

A *'supernatural supercollider'* created an *'im-plosion that ex-ploded'* with a thunderous eruption of light. A sound and light show rolled out of eternity and continues until this very day as the cosmos races from its point of origin toward an infinite *'googolplex'* [2] + 1 distance. For we earthlings, it is unreachable because, when you believe you have arrived at the end, there is always a +1 known only by Elyon.

BANG, BIG BANG, a blast from eternity! The explosive noise of creation was the *'Utterance (Word)'* of Elyon. *'Divine decibels'* that none but ♍ could hear, made for a resounding roar of preposterous proportion defying all description. *'The Beginning birthed by God!'* This is Genesis one from the Holy Bible, the Yugas of the Hindus, the Aboriginal Dream Time, the Ying and Yang of the Chinese. Elyon is creating the heavens and the earth! Alas, *'Emit'* was underway! Massive constellations, unnamed creatures, microscopic cells, things

1 Deep thoughts or meditations. Akin to Logos.

2 Milton Sirotta, coined the term googol, which is then proposed the further term googolplex to be "one, followed by writing zeroes until you get tired." Infinity!

seen and unseen materialized faster than time itself!

Most of what we know of this era comes from *"light fossils,"*[1] recently researched by the powerful Planck telescope. In some unexplainable way, Elyon created ♍-self. The *'Naught became a Number, the Only became the Alpha, the Alone became The Aleph*[2]*, the Eternal became The First, The Lone will be the Last."* All of this without giving up any of ♍ Godhood. However, every Alpha coexists with a companion Omega, every Aleph its Tav[3] and every First and Last. However, we are not to dwell on finalities or finishes here. Elyon is just getting started with ♍ creation that many of us have not considered. This contemplation will take us *'Where only Angels have dared to tread!'*

1 Light fossils - Ancient light dating to the "beginning." The 'afterglow of creation.' - Commonly known as cosmic background radiation.

2 First letter of the Jewish alphabet.

3 Last letter of the Jewish alphabet.

The Prodigal Satan

PLOT COUPON THREE
THE PATERNITY OF ETERNITY

The Eternal Elyon, the 'It' of Plot Coupon One, can now be considered as what we earthlings call Father. Of note, only humans call Elyon their Father; whereas Celestial beings address as "HOLY." We consider Holy to be an adjective that describes one's Divine character, but it can be an ethereal noun. In Creation, The 'Paternity of Eternity' became reality as ♍ made Son's ♎.[1] *That an angel was created without a mother of itself is paternalism to a miraculous degree. Then how much more incredible is the notion of the eternal Elyon being birthed by an earthly mother? The creator becoming a supernatural seed in the womb of ♍ creation? Considering such mysteries, how fully can created beings know their creator? Can we communicate with ♍? Can we see ♍? The Holy Scriptures inform us that angels can see the 'face of Elyon,'*[2] *but what else does ancient sources tell us about the existence of these beings?*

I propose that angels are everlasting beings, possessing indestructible spirits, although they, like we humans have destructible bodies. They function under a hierarchy of rules that subordinates them into classes and kinds. They are inquisitive and experience emotions. They eat, drink, sing, play musical instruments and dance. Angels are powerful, much more so than humans.[3] They are endowed with the ability to heal and to destroy. Unfortunately, they can be deceitful and

1 ♎ symbol for "He, She, Him or Her, Hers or His, Son(s) or Daughter(s)" The gender of Angels is unknown.

2 Matthew 18:10 - "See that you do not despise one of these little ones. For I tell you that their angels in heaven always see the face of my Father in heaven."

3 Psalms 8:5 - "Thou has made Him a little lower than the angels."

be deceived with deadly consequences!

Shockingly, Angels are sexually oriented beings! We are told that they don't marry in Vilon[1] as we do on earth. Marriage[2] is not mandated in a sinless society where no extramarital affairs exist. No fornication is found there! *'There are no celestial celibates!'* Even Elyon *'married Israel'*[3] and ♈ has a *'bride.'*[4]

1 The 7th heaven. Isaiah 40:22 - Vilon is "That stretches out the heavens as a curtain (Vilon), and spreads them out as a tent to dwell in." It is the entire universe, going beyond what we can see with telescopes.

2 Matthew 22:30 - "At the resurrection people will neither marry nor be given in marriage; they will be like the angels in heaven."

3 Jeremiah 3:14 - "Return o backslidden children, saith the Lord, for I am married to you."

4 Revelation 19:7 - "Let us rejoice and exult and give him the glory, for the marriage of the Lamb has come, and his Bride has made herself ready..."

PLOT COUPON FOUR
THE SONG THAT SHARES THE SECRET

Colossians 1:15-17 -"He is the image of the invisible God, <u>the firstborn</u> over all creation, for all things in heaven and on earth were created by him. All things, whether visible or invisible, whether thrones or dominions, whether principalities or powers. All things were created through him and for him. He himself is before all things and all things are held together in him."

Now we focus on the greatest of all 'mysteries,' searching out the secret sealed up from the masses for millenniums. Colossians 1:15-17 is considered by some to be *'an early Christian hymn'* sung by the early Christians as they congregated. Who is this *'He'* of the Colossians church? He is the invisible Elyon becoming visible to men. Under a canopy of stars stationed over Bethlehem, the angels gazed at us as we got our first glimpse of the Godhead in a goat shed? ♈ in a manger! Then they sang just as they had at creation.

A Roman born Hebrew Rabbi named Paul, the author of Colossians, identified Christ as the *"prototokos,"* the Greek word for *'firstborn.'* How can *'One'* born in AD three be the firstborn of all creation? What about the Angels, Adam or Abraham?

How could Jesus The Christ declare, "Before Abraham, I Am?"[1] The answer lies in the fact that The Eternal Elyon is not under the constraints of time as we are. *'Elyon has no yesterdays, no tomorrows, no past nor a future, only a forever.'* ♑ mocks time by calling our day a thousand years. AD three was two thousand years ago to us, but two days ago

1 1 John 8:58 - "Very truly I tell you," Jesus answered, "before Abraham was born, I am!"

to God using His *'jesting estimation.'* ♈ dwells in an *'Eternal Now.'* Sing early Christians sing! Sing modern Christians sing! Sing Angels sing! Sing all creation sing! Sing to the Firstborn!

It was an operation so surreptitious that only a *'supernatural psyche'* could have planned it. Just consider the verses and the chorus of this *'ancient anthem.'* "He is the image of the invisible, He is the Firstborn, He created all things visible or invisible, everything belongs to Him, He is before all things!" ♈ is the Firstborn, but a virgin teenager gave birth to ♈. ♈ created woman so that a woman could gestate and deliver ♈.

We have no idea of the scope and spectrum of what ♈ created because some of what ♈ made is invisible. From *'amoebae to the Andes, molecules to mountains, every planet, star, hill and valley, everything animate or inanimate, every plant, person or animal was made for His perusal and pleasure.'* Who among us would not want to be ♈, unless it happens to be crucifixion day of Passover A.D. 33!

This story begins and ends, primarily focusing on two main characters; Yeshua,[1] The Firstborn, The only begotten Son of Elyon and second, Satan, one of the created *'sons of Elyon.'* The unbegotten son demanded what did not, does not and will never belong to him. ♎ seeks to steal, kill and destroy[2] the *'Bequeathed inheritance of The begotten'*!

1 Yeshua - Hebrew word spelled Jesus in Greek.

2 John 10:10 - "The thief comes only to steal and kill and destroy."

PLOT COUPON FIVE
EMIT - AN EVENT WHO'S TIME HAD NOT COME

Emit was not some random, chaotic happening. It was not a freak 'combination of chemicals' that by happenstance caused the epic event we call creation. 'Creation was not a cosmic accident.' It was envisioned, arranged, organized and orderly. Everything came into existence by design, drafted by the Logos; it's size measured, it's colors chosen, it's place positioned, it's name selected, it's rank assigned. No detail was overlooked, 'every constellation, comet, star, sun, planet, meteor or asteroid was given a name[1] and set on a course.' Just as all created beings have a specific purpose and assignment, so do bodies of Rakia[2].

Consider the Earth; the Crown Jewel among the planetary masses of which we have knowledge. Just think, the "Terra Firma" is perfectly positioned on it polar axis; safely situated a precise safe distance from its Sun and minutely measured away from its moon. Everything is exactly arranged for its existence! Earth's assignment is to serve as *'the stage upon which the Drama of all ages is being acted out.'* This is not to suggest that there in nothing else of value in other galaxies. If there should be, it all belongs to the Firstborn and is ♈ inheritance. *'Value is ascribed to things according to the amount of attention affixed on them.'* Case closed! Elyon

1 Psalms 147:4 - "He keeps track of the number of stars, assigning names to all of them."

2 Genesis 1:17 tells of the 6th Heaven! Rakia is where 'God set celestial bodies in the firmament (Rakia) of the heavens.' This is a reference to the stars, sun, moon, and planets: outer space where the various heavenly bodies move in their prescribed orbits and/or maintain relationships in constellations, solar systems, galaxies, etc. Rakia is the part of the heavens that can be seen.

has a fixation and it is the Earth, the only Planet mentioned as created with the heavens in Genesis 1:1. What is the meaning of the Special mention? Hmmm!

The Prodigal Satan

PLOT COUPON SIX
ROMANCING THE STONES

Job 38:4-7 - "Where were you when I laid the foundation of the earth? Tell me, if you have understanding. Who determined its measurements—surely you know! Or who stretched the line upon it? On what were its bases sunk, or who laid its cornerstone when the morning stars sang together and all the sons of God shouted for joy?"

Six of Elyon's first words recorded are, "Let There Be" and "It Is Good." At the speaking of these words, all the created beings vigorously applauded or so the earliest translations of Job thirty-eight suggest, "all the sons of God 'clapped' for Joy." Why is this fact mentioned? The Origin of the word Explosion is a Latin word, *"Explosio"* meaning the act of clapping. We understand that the Angels were created with a *'Divine discharge of dunumos.'*[1]

In other words, they *'came like a clap of thunder.'* The angels were stupefied by the reality of their own existence, but it paled in comparison to their marveling as they beheld *'the Majesty of their Maker.'*

There was no doubt concerning where they came from and to whom they owed their existence! Simultaneous with the clapping, the sound of 'viols'[2] was heard as *'music'* melodiously flowed out of tubes[3] jutting from the innermost center of certain of the angels. Science has proven that light makes music by emitting electronically produced particles as does the Aurora Borealis in Earth's northern atmospheric

1 Greek word for power. English word dynamite.

2 Viols - stringed instrument like in Violin.

3 Ezekiel 28:13 - "The workmanship of thy tabrets and of thy pipes was prepared in thee in the day that thou wast created."

hemisphere. Recently, satellites recorded the sound of 'stars singing'! The *'light beings'* rejoiced in amazement. Maon's melodies co-mingled with clapping and music set to the words Holy, Agios,[1] Qadash![2]

As a *'plethora of the pious angelic population'* worshiped, they realized that something selectively special was underway. One of the Chayot took the lead and roared out an invitation to the others, as ♎ shouted, "Come and see." Every created being careened to catch a glimpse of *'project planet, planned and prefabricated by Elyon, now in production.'* At Bene Elyon's command, *'framing materials'* reporting for work as *'Construction Comets'* came calling, eager to find their place and part in the formation of Earth. Elyon spoke and ♍ voice was recognized as the vocabulary of the elements iron, silicon, magnesium, sulfur, nickel, calcium and aluminum; our seven major elements. Each of the respective elements relocated to the strata selected as their station on the pristine planet Earth. Then for decoration, ♍ sprinkled in trace amounts of platinum, gold, silver and many other agates, amethyst, sapphires, emeralds, rubies, pearls, jasper, topaz and lastly, one called *'girls best friend,'* the diamonds.

Smaller stones were crafted by the *'Divine Designer'* and shrewdly sown into the angelic bodies as decorations *'demon-striating'*[3] the depth of inner spirits. It is plausible to propose, the bodies of the angels are created from the same *"space dust"* which concentrated, forming the crust of earth. Angels are like we humans, constructed of the same elements, but favorably fashioned above us.

1 Agios - Holy in Greek.

2 Qadash - Holy in Hebrew. The Angel's native tongue is unknown!

3 Ezekiel 28:13 - "Every precious stone was thy covering, the sardius, topaz, and the diamond, the beryl, the onyx, and the jasper, the sapphire, the emerald, and the carbuncle, and gold."

The Prodigal Satan

Doubtless, the creatures were overwhelmed with awestruck wonder as Elyon rolled out a measure, stretched a line and laid the foundation of the Earth. Also present were creatures called *'Morning Stars'*[1] being part of the *'first tranche of creation,'* they were advanced in rank, second only to the Godhead and especially gifted to sing. So sing they did! Astonishment erupted into yet another round of rapturous applause, commensurate to the monumental moment they witnessed. Their creation song included a familiar rendition of "Holy, Holy, Holy," but they added a chorus, "Lord Elyon Almighty, who Was, Who Is and is ever coming."[2] Everything was perfect and in harmonious alignment. The Love affair was in full bloom!

1 Job 38:7 - "When the morning stars sang together..."

2 Revelation 4:8 - "Holy, holy, holy, is the Lord God Almighty, who was and is and is to come!"

PLOT COUPON SEVEN
HEAVEN'S MATHEMATICS

Psalms 147:4 - "He counts the number of the stars. He calls them all by their names!"

This ancient scripture is translated four ways, He tells, He appoints, He determines, He counts. All of these words are indicators of mathematical interaction. Numbers are indicative of Elyon's code of conduct (ethos). It has to be so, for numbers are the one constant that we know to be like ♍, in that they are invariable and immutable. They are fixed and do not fluctuate. The angels watched as Elyon *'measured, marked, weighed, used scales and a balance.'* "Who has measured the waters in the hollow of his hand, or with the breadth of his hand marked off Vilon? Who has held the dust of the Earth in a basket, or weighed the mountains on the scales and the hills in a balance?"[1]

We humans have learned math, but Elyon is Math. ♍ alone possesses the knowledge of what is beyond plus one. (+1). Choose your highest number and then add one more and you have a new higher number, making math endless, even as Elyon is endless. Elyon's mathematical system placed the earth, sun and moon, as we know them now, at determined distances from one another and in perfect proportion to one another. The earth's sun is a G-type main sequence star. This class of star is mostly stable so its fluctuations are not measurably enough to destroy life on this planet. As the moon orbits earth, it exerts pressure on the crust of the earth and the oceans. This causes tides to rise and fall, cleaning out the

1 Isaiah 40:12 – "Who has measured the waters in the hollow of his hand, or with the breadth of his hand marked off the heavens? Who has held the dust of the earth in a basket, or weighed the mountains on the scale and the hills in a balance?

rivers and streams. Without movement, water would become too polluted to support life. If the moon were any nearer to earth, the outer crust would erupt causing severe earthquakes every time it orbited the Planet. The tides would rise too high and take most of the land mass into the sea. The moon also causes the tilt of the earth's axis to an exacting point, which allows for us to have seasonal changes. This is necessary for plants to live and grow. Here is some amazing arithmetic! The distance between the moon and the sun is 400 times greater than the distance from the earth and the moon. The Sun happens to be 400 times the Moon's diameter, and 400 times as far away. *"Is this mathematics meted out in meticulous metrics or merely accidental arithmetic?"*

The Prodigal Satan

PLOT COUPON EIGHT
HEAVEN'S MESSAGE

"God created everything by number, weight and measure." (Newton)

Isaiah 55:9 - "The heavens are higher than the earth, so are my ways higher than your ways and my thoughts than your thoughts."

For those of us who do not understand the language of computer programming, tellingly named "Python," even though it is at its core composed of a conglomeration of first graders 0's and 1's. It is conceivable that there is a message scripted in Rakia that can be deciphered by mortals. 'Planets are God pencils to write His Word.' Think of it as 'God's Galactic glottology'[1] written as a witness of Elyon's willingness to communicate 'a meteorological message to His creation.' I will not go into what the astrologers, necromancers, soothsayers and witches who have wished what 'The Message' would be. However, long before there was 'Oral Tradition," 'A Babel-ing Tower, a 'Written language, or an Angel preaching another Gospel,' there was this, "For the director of music. A psalm of David. The heavens declare the glory of God; the skies proclaim the work of his hands."[2] This is ♍ language, linguistically perfect for 'Garden residents, nomadic tent dwellers and shepherds abiding in the fields'. Anyone living beneath *'Elyon's blackboard'* can study the stars as they serve as *'evening educators'* in *'God's Night School 101.'* Elyon would not leave his creation without excuse, so Rakia became ♍ *'show and tell,'* replete with flash card stars, some shooting and others stationary, like the dots and dashes of *'a majestic*

1 The science of tongues and languages.

2 Psalms 19:1

Morse code,' communicating ♍ message of revelation, rebellion, redemption and restoration!

As it was, is and will be until the finish, other powers usurp, undermine and seek to avert the ambitions of the *'Almighty Author'* of the heavens. Please *'don't dare to trust the tainted tea leaves of the Tempter.' 'Satan's horoscope is just that, a scope of horror'* that leads to false readings, fake religion and fatal results. The Satan that I am introducing is a seducer, a spoiler and a serpent. This *'strangling python'* possesses the bodies of men and beasts by poisoning their spirits as ♎ peddles ♎ perjury against the True Elyon!

PLOT COUPON NINE
HEAVEN'S DEMOGRAPHICS

It is time to introduce you to our cast of characters! Our first observation is that not one of Elyon's creatures was created as Demons. Elyon did not create evil. Evil is "a bastard of its own breed and brand." There is 'no father in the family tree of falsehood.' Becoming a devil is a matter of choice and will. Our first and foremost actor is the antithesis of a demon. He is the Christ, the 'Anointed Aleph,' the Firstborn, the Only Begotten Son Of God.

Satan is Second, *'The Progenitor of Poison, the Belligerent Bet, Lucifer the Lesser,'* a created son of God. It is necessary for us to investigate the hierarchy of Angels, if we are to realize the full import of this saga. At some point, past, present or future, each kind and species of supernatural beings will admirably or adversely affect the heavens, the earth and eternity. The names of the various actor angels will be revealed as our story begins to unfold.

First, is *Bene Elohim* (♈) The Begotten Son of Elyon. The "Firstborn of all creation." Also known as the "Angel of the Lord" in the Old Testament of the Holy Bible.

The Prodigal Satan

Second in rank and order are the Chayot, the living beings exhibiting the shape of a man, with four faces, that of man, lion, ox and eagle, having four wings; They glow like burning coals, having calf's feet that sparkle like brass as they travel like lightning.[1]

1 Ezekiel 1:7 - "And their feet were straight feet; and the sole of their feet was like the sole of a calf's foot: and they sparkled like the color of burnished brass."

Third are Ophanim, who are identified as a class of celestial beings in later sections of the Book of Enoch as being with the Cherubim and Seraphim, who never sleep, but perpetually guard the throne of God. They are the eye-covered four wheels that move next to the winged Cherim beneath the throne of Elyon. They are filled with the spirit of the Cherubim and dutifully transport the throne of Elyon, wherever the spirit of The Cherubim is directed to go.

The Prodigal Satan

Fourth are Erelim or perhaps as we will then suggest, a singular being of special status. One creature closely associated with the earth. "Azazel" is called an ancient name for the Leontomorphic (lionlike), Gnostic Demiurge (Creator God). Others have dubbed Azazel as "Earth's great lord, 'spirit of air, angel of the waters of the Earth and wielder of fire." In mysticism, Azazel is usually considered as a governing angel with dominion over the Earth, creative forces, the North, elemental spirits, and beasts. Most evil comes with an alias, masks and a multitude of costumes in which they seek to hide their true identity.

The Prodigal Satan

Hashmallim in the Hebrew Bible in Ezekiel 1:4- "I saw, and behold, there was a stormy wind coming from the north, a great cloud with flashing fire and a brilliant light surrounding it; and from its midst, like the color of Hashmal (Tarnished green copper) from the midst of the fire, and in its midst there was the likeness of four Chayot (living creatures).

Sixth are the Seraphim who are literally, "burning ones." The word seraph is a synonym for serpents when used in the Hebrew Bible. Isaiah 6:1-8 used the term to describe fiery six-winged beings who fly around God's throne saying, "Holy, Holy, Holy."

Seventh, Malakim are Messengers who serve as angelic envoys.

Eight, the Elohim are a plethora of godly beings, that are delegated to wholly represent deity and as such were called gods.

Ninth, this order belongs to the *Cherubim* who are guardians of God's glory.

Tenth, the Malakim are *'angelic manlike beings.'*[1]

"And God said They were Good."

1 Genesis 18:2 - "Abraham looked up and saw three men standing nearby." (Angels)

Daniel 10:5 - "I looked up and there before me was a man dressed in linen, with a belt of fine gold from Uphaz around his waist."

The Prodigal Satan

PLOT COUPON TEN
HEAVEN'S MESSENGERS AND MENACES

On this side of eternity, we may never know the real names of the spirits that we now call 'demons.' As most criminals do, they change their names and identities. Contrariwise, there are many beings that we can positively identify as the Archangels of the highest order. They rule over the affairs of men at the bequest of The Christ; namely Gabriel, Michael, Raphael and Uriel, Raguel, Remiel and Saraqael. Several others include Satan of The Order of The Erelim, Beelzebub,[1] *and Leviathan.*

Starting with Gabriel, consider the complex creatures created by Elyon for ♍ service. Gabriel is exceptional in that we are given a description of ♎ in the Holy Scriptures. We are told that ♎ is gargantuan in girth and height likely towering over every other species. His body, given in biblical terms, looks like lightning.

As we will learn, Satan's body produced music, likewise Gabriel's body generated *'cosmic currents'* unknown to we mortals. Imagine the stealth of movement possessed by this mighty *'light-being,'* knowing that *'light-ning'* travels faster than sound. One plausible explanation for ♎ energy extraordinaire is that ♎ *'harnessed light'* powers the *'laser like'* weapons that ♎ wields. The ancients who beheld Gabriel's visitations, dared to describe ♎ weapon as a *"flaming sword"* and ♎ vehicles as *'chariots of fire.'* They were likely searching for words, just as I am now, to describe supernatural happenings, based upon their personal experiences and encounters.

Gabriel is also empowered with special gifts and ♎

1 Beelzebub - In Hebrew lord of the flies.

is privy to the plans, programs and purposes of Elyon. This established ♎ in an exalted position of leadership among the angelic hierarchy. ♎ is not omniscient, but is directly linked to the Word (Logos) and is trusted to thoroughly communicate *'the thoughts of Theos'*[1] without pause or prevarication. Satan especially envies Gabriel, because of ♎ (Gabriel's) especial endowment from the Holy One. Satan disregards order or rank unless it is ♎ who takes ownership or rules. ♎ desires to control principalities and to preside over all others and would succeed if not hindered by the likes of Gabriel the Archangel of God.

Michael came into being enabled with exceeding strength and power. What ♎ lacks in size is supplemented by ♎ superior strength. Our *'Angelic Atlas'* is *'the Supernatural Sergeant at Arms, Heaven's Bailiff, an Ethereal Enforcer.'* Even ♎ countenance contorts with clues of ♎ potency and power. The glare of ♎ eyes blaze like burning torches and the sternness shown in his set jaw is telling. In other words, Michael is dreadfully dangerous to any who dare defy ♎! None but Satan would dare to challenge ♎, or to reject the demands of *'the Deity who deputized Michael.'* Michael can wrest with the worst of the wicked ones and always win. At ♎ appearance it must be announced, "Fear Not." ♎ arrival always caused *'angels to quiver, shepherds to shake. Kings fell on their faces like slaves before ♎ while others behaved as dead men.'* Michael truly is the *'Prevailing Power'* among the Princes of heaven, the *'Leader of the Legions'* among angels! ♎ possesses the power to shut and open the doors of Shechakim[2] or arrest and chain the darkest of powers in the

1 Theos - Greek word for God - Root of the word theology, the study of God.

2 The Fifth Heaven Shechakim is Elyon's Storehouse of Supernatural goods. Psalm 78:23 - "He commanded the skies (shechakim) above and opened the doors of heaven; and He rained down manna upon them to eat."

deepest dug pit.

Raphael is prepared for perpetuating the peace of Zevul, Machon[1] and Aravot.[2] ♎ is unmistakably recognizable seeing ♎ appearance is as radiant as a prism. ♎ internal rainbow disperses its promising light in every direction. Raphael's glow of peaceful colors sends light waves of calm into every realm ♎ enters.

Elyon never intended for there to be confusion in ♍ celestial courts or Earthly cities. So, such is the calling of Raphael, to secure the serenity of the heavens and earth. ♎ is given great power to purify, whether the contamination is animate or inanimate; to keep the atmosphere crystal clear and the waters of the firmament pure. Included in Raphael's repertoire is the ability to cleanse the spirits of men, beasts or angels. So if it be the healing of polluted waters or the putrid heart of man, the cure lies within the power of this peaceful Prince of angels. Unfortunately, Raphael's greatest challenge is Satan, who sadly is so sick with sedition that no salve can affect ♎ cure. Satan's open and oozing sore of discontentment drives ♎ vitriol hatred to become hopelessly harmful and timelessly terminal. Satan as a prodigal seeks to waste the bountiful beauty of God's handiwork and turn it into a cesspool of uncleanness and corruption.

Uriel is an Ophanim entrusted with *'she-kinah;'* a *'Special Light,'* second only to the *'True Light'* of *'The Holy One.'* The facade of Uriel's face and the breadth of ♎ body are fascinating. Notable features include multiple eyes round

1 The second heaven Machon is the location of the storehouse of Natural goods. 1 Kings 8:39 - "The Lord shall open unto you His good treasure…"
Deuteronomy 28:12 - "We know that this is heaven because 'Hear in Heaven, the habitation '(Machon)' of Your dwelling…."

2 The First Heaven '(Aravot).' This is the atmosphere that surrounds the Earth in which Humans, animals and angels can live. Psalm 68:4 - "Cast up a highway for Him Who rides upon the clouds. (Aravot) His name is Yah."

about as in a wheel, adequately equipping ♎ to accomplish ♎ assignment. Nothing important can be hidden from this one's insight. Multi-faceted eyes provide ♎ hindsight and foresight. Uriel incessantly monitors *'the intensity of illumination'* in all of God's creatures that ♎ may bestow healing and restoration to them. If one's luster lessens to any degree, Uriel comes to share the *'she-kinah'* in a caring fashion that is tantamount to what we humans relate to as a Mother's love. Interestingly, the word Shekinah is a feminine word and it speaks to the nurturing nature of ♍.[1] Like a Mother, Uriel can see hurts that others overlook and then set about to heal them all.

When a humans skin turns ashen grey, their loss of luminance is symptomatic of something we humans call sickness. In the heavens, darkness is diagnosed as a curse common to the DNA of its *'carrier,'* namely Satan, who is also known as The Devil, *'The Looter of light,'* and *'The Rustler of radiance.'*

The Hashmallim Raguel is Elyon's appointee to administer the Justice of God, acting as *'Jehovah's Judge'* in angelic matters. No one knows what ♎ body looks like except for ♎ face. It is like unto the face of an eagle. ♎ left eye seeps trickling tears even as ♎ right eye pierces the core of every creature. Otherwise there is no expression on ♎ face; *'no smile or sorrow, no fear nor favor, just the blank stare of justice'* betrayed only by tears for those who are on the wrong side of Elyon's laws. When administering justice Raguel lifts ♎ pinions to reveal a body covered by a reflecting robe of silver. Any one seeking justice is seen outwardly and inwardly, but most importantly, they see their selves in the mirror of Raguel's robe. What greater picture of Justice could there be? Though Raguel is one of the *'Covering Angels,'* it

1 Isaiah 66:13 - As a mother comforts her child, so will I comfort you; and you will be comforted over Jerusalem."

may shock your sensibility to learn that one of ♎ partnering *"Coverers"* was Satan! Together, they covered the seat of power (throne) in Zevul[1]. The covering angels spread their pinions over the Heavenly Ark of Elyon's Covenant that contains the *'Law Journals of Jehovah.'* The *'coverers'* incessantly recite the regal rules and regulations for the remembrance of those who serve the regime of heaven. Satan proved, *'to recite to others is not evidence that a catechism is the conviction of the cantor.'*

Ramiel the Cherubim is stationed alongside the most strategic place in all of heaven, next to the Mercy Seat in the epicenter of Elyon's Throne. ♎ assignment is to allocate Mercy to the souls who acknowledge their need of it. This angel's appearance is different from the other bright, translucent beings. ♎ coloration is a comely crimson red, resembling a glowing ember of fire. ♎ hue is similar to the color of fresh flowing human blood, which would prove to be prophetic. Red is the color of redemption.[2] One would suppose that Ramiel is the busiest of all of Elyon's agents, but it just isn't so. Sadly, ♎ has the most to offer and the fewest takers. Mercy can only be shown to those who are willing to give it. One of the great blessings of all ages goes as follows, "Blessed are the merciful, for they shall obtain mercy."[3] Where have all the merciful gone?

Ramiel will eventually be appointed to fly through Maon[4] and Aravot, crying out Elyon's message of mercy, only

1 The 4th Heaven. Zevul is the location of celestial Jerusalem and the temple with the heavenly altar. 1 Kings 8:13 - "I have surely built you a house of habitation. (Zevul), a place for you to dwell in forever." Isaiah 63:16 - "Look down from heaven and behold the habitation (Zevul) of Your holiness and Your glory."

2 Hebrews 9:22 - "Without the shedding of blood there is no forgiveness for sin."

3 Matthew 5:7 - "Blessed are the merciful: for they shall obtain mercy."

4 The Third Heaven Maon. This is where His ministering angels stay, singing in

to bear the brunt of unrequited love from many of Satan's demons destined for damnation. ♎ will fly yet a second time with a similar message.[1] We call ♎ *'The Minister of Mercy, Ramiel the rejected, The frustrated flyer.'*

The Chayot Saraquel has four faces, as ♎ stands in the presence of Elyon, superintending every aspect of angelic activity. ♎ is called The *"Angel of Presence"* [2] and comes alongside the other *'Powers'* to assist in their assignments. Since none are supposed to fully behold the "glory" of God.

It is the distinct honor of Saraquel to display the characteristics of God. One of the faces is that of a Lion. The Lion being King over all the natural creatures speaks to the fact that God and God alone is King over everything and everyone created, both natural and supernatural.

Of all the faces, Satan most admires the Lion. Its ability to paralyze it prey with its mighty roar and tear it asunder with one swipe of its sharp claws, appeals to heavens 'Murderous Menace.'

The second face of Saraquel is that of an eagle. Winged angels pay special attention to feathered flyers as they curiously watch eagles venture into the heights of Aravot, bordering on breaking through unseen barriers that God has set for every living thing. The angels feel very akin to the eagles due to their resemblance to them and their ability to command the sky. Whereas the other creatures of the Chayot are bound to plod and prowl on the surface of the stones.

The message of the Eagle is, God soars far above every

the night. We know that this is heaven. Deuteronomy 26:15 - "Look down from your holy habitation (Maon) from heaven."

1 Revelation 14:6 - "And I saw another angel fly in the midst of heaven, having the everlasting gospel to preach unto them that dwell on the earth...."

2 Isaiah 63:9 - "In all their distress he too was distressed, and the angel of his presence saved them."

other creature that ♍ made. None can surpass ♍.

The third observance is the face of an ox, the strongest of all natural creatures, which certainly means that God is omnipotent, unsurpassed in strength.

The Man like fourth face mystifies the angels. It is a striking resemblance to that of Yeshua. Even its name *'Man'* is a mystery. Perhaps Elyon included ♍-self in the design of the strangest of all ♍ creatures; *'The Chayot.'*

As the angelic voices chorused Holy, Holy, Holy, the resounding roar of the lion, the piercing cry of the eagle and the bellowing of the ox was heard in unison throughout the heavens. Much to the confusion and consternation of Satan, the voice of the Man like beast remained mute. Why did the Man like face not offer up praise to Elyon? If indeed the Man's face is the face of ♈, would not the Son of Elyon have to praise Elyon or is ♈ Elyon? As the Lion, the Eagle and the Ox are the greatest of their kind, so is ♈ King over everything.[1] Satan envies ♈, and lusts after his exemption from praise and worship. ♎ also frets that the fourth face is part of the puzzle of the Godhead.

1 Ephesians 1:22 - "God placed all things under His feet."

The Prodigal Satan

PROLOGUE TWO

Isaiah 45:18 - "for thus saith the Lord that created (bara - to create a new thing) the heavens; God himself that formed (yatsar - to mould into a form, as a potter does) the earth and made (asah, to fashion, prepare) it; he hath established (kun, to form) it, he created (bara) it not in vain (tohu, ruin), he formed (yatsar) it to be inhabited."

If all the heavens were somehow googled and mapped, then you entered the word *'throne,'* you could spend countless hours watching your computerized device zoom through cyberspace, back to before time began and your light emitting diode Windows[1] would finally focus in on an object bigger that anything seen by you or 'Hubble' until now. It is so big that present day astronomers would have to recalculate their theories concerning the creation that they don't believe in. If you expanded your search to include the words, Throne/Satan you would be transported back beyond time, into the inter-sanctum of a gargantuan Throne. There you would see Satan[2] with ♎ pinions uplifted over a indescribable rectangular object covered with stones and inscriptions. Satan is accompanied by Raguel[3] as they cautiously cover this object, dutifully guarding the Glory of Elyon. Satan, Raguel's co-coverer was a cause for concern, considering ♎ demeanor. ♎ displayed the behavior of a Devil in the making.

'It is Satan who caused the heavenly defection, devising dishonesty, distortion and defamation of Elyon.'

Who could Raguel report to that had the authority to do anything about the developing difficulty? Besides, the

1 Trademarked by Microsoft.

2 Satan - A Erelim. An Angel of opposition. The Adversary.

3 Raguel - A Cherubim. An Angel of Justice and Judgment.

creatures could hear the voice of Elyon, but they were not allowed to speak back or to Elyon. Only Bene Elyon (♈) possessed permission to address the Almighty for He was the Almighty. Yes, God talks to ♍-self! [1]

This created a dilemma for Raguel because ♈ is the only One who can deal with discord, which is one of the six things God Hates.[2]

Are angels to praise Elyon continually? "Yes!" Glorify ♍ eternally? "Yes!" When Elyon speaks a command, the creatures are only allowed the prerogative of replying affirmatively. It is unilaterally and unquestionably understood, "YES" is the only acceptable answer. The concept of "No" does not exist.

As Elyon spoke, Raguel watched Satan's lips moving in a fashion that seemed strange. No sounds came out, but Satan's scowling expression spoke loud enough to make ♎ heard. A silent "No" reverberated throughout every region of the heavens. 'The Rebellion' was underway!

1 Psalms 33:11 - "The Godhead speaks to itself and seeks its own council."

2 Proverbs 6:16-19 - "These six things the Lord hates, Yes, seven are an abomination to Him: A proud look, A lying tongue, Hands that shed innocent blood, A heart that devises wicked plans, Feet that are swift in running to evil, A false witness who speaks lies, And one who sows discord among brethren."

The Prodigal Satan

CHAPTER ONE
THE SEDITIOUS SECRET OF SATAN

Ezekiel 28:15 & 17 - "You were blameless in your ways from the day you were created, till unrighteousness was found in you. Your heart was proud because of your beauty; you corrupted your wisdom for the sake of your splendor."

Other than the scowling look of repugnance on Satan's extraordinarily beautiful face, there were few things that concerned Raguel. There were some Angels, whose behavior seemed suspect, but in the sterile serenity of The Heavens where tranquility had never been tested, trust reigned supreme and trepidation was scarce. The angels were only allowed to converse among their selves and to use the gift of words that Elyon taught them. Since Elyon named everything that existed, no words other than those in ♍ vocabulary were ever spoken. Recently, Raguel overheard several other Seraphim's, one named Beelzebub[1] and another Leviathan,[2] speaking strange words. ♎ sensed that their intent was to conceal some secret.

"Beelzebub, Leviathan come closer lest Raguel hear me," Satan softly whispered. "I will tell you hidden things that even the Holy One does not know."

Satan was taking a huge risk, doing something unprecedented with unknown consequences! The shock of ♎ statement sent a shiver among the angels, chilling the fire and light beings.

Satan tenuously continued, "Beelzebub, tell me if I am wrong but you and I seem so alike. It is though we are one. Then you, Leviathan, I have watched you; how you are

1 Beelzebub - A Hashmallim, Angel of rank over the heights of heaven.

2 Leviathan - A Seraphim, Angel of rank over the lower levels of heaven.

a leader of great influence." Beelzebub and Leviathan were anxious about nodding their approval of Satan's admiration!

Upon seeing the nods, Satan became bolder, "Leviathan, the Malakim watch you and emulate your every move." In unison, Beelzebub and Leviathan bowed before Satan to acknowledge ♎ cunning compliments.

"What would you have us to know that Elyon does not?" Leviathan solemnly solicited. ♎ golden yellow eyes skeptically searched Satan's serene face for any sign of deceit. "Tell us, tell us now," ♎ added.

Satan could not have hoped for more. A powerful leader such as Leviathan lending support to ♎ cause was critical!

Leviathan's question was the perfect response. It was an unholy reply that told Satan, Leviathan was open to challenge Elyon's omniscience.

"Could it be that Elyon really is not all knowing and that ♍ is really just like the rest of us?" Satan quickly added. ♎ felt strengthened considering a Seraphim of great influence would choose to articulate such a convincing argument.

Not to be left out Beelzebub conjectured, "If we indeed are the Sons of Elyon, then we too are gods, in every way equal to any other god."

'A trinity of truth breakers' was formed in that moment. Two powerful angels became *'demonic allies'* with the one whose evil eclipsed all the others. These three knew of Elyon's sacred word, *'Covenant.'* This word is indelibly inscribed on all sides of Elyon's Throne.

Satan seized the moment, suggesting, "We three should make our own covenant. You Beelzebub, Leviathan and me inseparable forever! Together, we will expose the falsehood of the so called Elyon and ♍ skewed supposition of a being the solitary supreme God. *It was indeed ironic, Covenant breakers becoming Covenant makers!"*

Leviathan agreed, "Why? Just tell me why Elyon should receive our unending praise? Do we not deserve the same adoration?"

Joyous laughter is commonplace in Maon, but this noise was different. It sounded suspiciously sinister as the conspirators squealed in delight at their self-aggrandizement.[1] The abnormality of their laughter arrested the attention of Raguel. The conniving trinity quickly quieted as Beelzebub noticed Raguel and Uriel[2] staring in their direction, their amber like eyes flashing inquisitively. Now, it was Satan's turn to shiver, causing ♎ to fling ♎ long black cape around ♎ thin torso. ♎ supposed that their subversive conversation had been observed and overheard. "Shush, quiet, not now," Satan hissed as he raised ♎ bony finger to ♎ ebony lips.

1 Arrogance or egotism

2 Uriel is an Ophanim, a "seer," He is a great light, known as "the watching angel that can reveal and heal."

The Prodigal Satan

CHAPTER TWO
DEMONIC DIALECT

John 8:44 - "You belong to your father, the devil, and you want to carry out your father's ... When he lies, he speaks his native language, for he is a liar and the father of lies."

It was too late to be silent, *'a demonic dialect, a tongue'* all of its own was spoken into existence. The first *'Ebonic,*[1] *mispronounced in heaven; a lect*[2] *laced with evil erupted with a seemingly simple word;' 'WHY?'*

Indeed Satan was right about being like Elyon in a sense. Using deceit, ♎ became a creator. Unfortunately for all creation, ♎ is *"the creator of chaos!"*

Uriel, as a guardian of the light was summoned to the scene. ♎ talent allowed ♎ to test the veracity of anything ♎ encountered by shining holy light into them. In this instance ♎ was reluctant to radiate ♎ Shekinah in the direction of three coequal beings as influential as Satan, Leviathan and Beelzebub. This could be risky without counseling with The Chayot.[3] Uriel very quietly queried, "Raguel, I suspicion, something never before done in heaven is happening over there."

Without hesitation, Raguel responded, "I see the situation the same as you and I know it is my place to pass judgment, but this seems most serious. We should seek council from the Chayot." A fleeting thought of doubt swept through Raguel. It was an uncomfortable sensation of guilt ♎ had never experienced and it was not to be entertained, but ♎ struggled to shake the unthinkable thought, the negative

1 A dialect or distinctive variety of speech.

2 Lect is much the same a dialect.

3 Chayot - Living beings with four faces.

notion, "Does Elyon really know about this without being told by us?" An inner voice perturbed Raguel. ♎ violently shook ♎ enormous head from side to side, hopeful of dislodging the thought, "If Elyon knows what Satan said, then ♍ knows what I just thought."

Little did ♎ know that a lethal "Why" had been released into the atmosphere. Like poisonous gas, it could disperse throughout heaven, threatening every creature! Raguel shuddered again as ♎ inner light visibly flickered and dimmed.

♎ dared not share ♎ experience with Uriel, but could not help but ask, "Uriel, did you see anything unusual happen to me?" Uriel was taken with the bizarre behavior of Satan. So, much to Raguel's relief, the answer was that ♎ had not noticed any thing.

Uriel suggested, "We should discuss this dilemma with Raphael."[1] This situation had the makings of a major mutiny, so they wisely summoned *'the specialist of serenity.'*

"Raphael, we are concerned that something is amiss among certain of the angels. "We saw...."

Raphael interrupted, "Are you going to speak to me about Satan?"

"Yes." "Why yes we are," Raguel replied in a shocked tone. "But how did you know?"

"This is not the first report that I have received concerning Satan." "I have been expecting to hear from you Raguel, seeing how intimately you served alongside Satan. My astonishment is that you didn't come to your conclusion long before now. I would have dealt with this situation but Ramiel[2] counseled me to be careful of accusations. I wanted to take up

1 Raphael - Angel of Peace and Serenity.

2 Ramiel - Angel of Mercy and Reconciliation.

my concerns with Saraquel,[1] but when we go to the 'Angel Of Presence...'

"Yes," Uriel interrupted, "I know, there can be no turning back. Do we know enough to go that far?" Raphael's face contorted with a look of concern over Uriel's comment. "Uriel, it is not what we know that matters. You believe that Elyon is *'all knowing'* and we are ♍ messengers mandated to do ♍ will."

Uriel felt ashamed of ♎ statement and silently worried, "Do I really trust that Elyon knows?"

Raphael curiously watched as Uriel departed, mumbling as ♎ went, "yes, yes, yes, yes, yes, yes, I believe."

A decision was made. Satan's damnable diatribe had to be disclosed and dealt with. The archangels would approach the Almighty.

1 Saraquel - The Angel of Presence.

CHAPTER THREE
THE PLOT DARKENS

Satan was savvy and ♎ concluded that a council was forthcoming and ♎ would not be caught unprepared. Leviathan and Beelzebub hastily began marshaling their commanders and the host of creatures under their charge.

Satan barked, "We will show them power." Forgetting that Elyon is math, ♎ and all numbers are known to ♍, ♎ blurted out, "Elyon has no notion of the hordes that will stand with me." Satan barked, "Beelzebub, Leviathan, go now to every *'bottle of the heavens'*[1] and tell the things that that you have learned. Preach that Elyon is not Holy. Sow discord by asking challenging questions! How can ♍ be holy as ♍ creates classes, subjugates us to one another, mainly to ♍-self? I tire of chanting Holy to my equal.

Tell the Malakim[2] of our plan, *"one heaven, one rank, one order, all things equal, and no one holy!"* This became *'the cry of their coupe de tat, the mantra of their madness!'*

Beelzebub and Leviathan joined with Satan to recruit other angels. Their rancor of their radical speeches not only riled up the angels, it repelled their light, allowing darkness to creep ever closer. Dark wisely disguised itself as a mixture of beautiful colors and hues which mesmerized the Malakim. At first, they thought the arrival of the colors to be Raphael coming to join their ranks. Raphael's appearance is that of the rainbows. The colors gradually layered one upon another,

1 Job 38:37 - "Who has the wisdom to count the clouds (Heavens)?" There are Seven Quadrants of Heaven. Heavens is always plural in Hebrew, with seven levels of heaven, noted in Scripture. The names are: Vilon, Rakia, Shechakim, Zevul, Maon, Machon, and Aravot.

2 Malakim - Messengers. A term used for Angels in general.

'merging into a murky magenta, progressing into a pigment possessing no light whatsoever!'

Every time Satan, Leviathan or Beelzebub voiced their vulgar message, questioning Elyon's authority, they enabled a darker shade of evil to emerge. The unbridled passion of Satan's believers so blinded them; none noticed the dusky discoloration settling in. Many angels in the audience were agape and stunned by the speeches of the angry Satan. Multitudes of the Malakim, angered by the growing anarchy, began incessantly chanting, "Holy, Holy, Holy."

The celestial regions reverberated with pathos as the pleadings of the righteous rivaled the *'hellish, howling heretics.'* The pious pinioned ones prayed that their passionate pleas would prevent what they perceived to be the end of their privileged existence. Their appeal to The Holy One seemed to have no effect, other than to incite and inspire the taunting trinity to continue their tirade.

Satan screamed all the louder hoping to drown out the Holy hymn of ♎ opposition. "As Satan hath said, How...?" Even louder ♎ chanted, "How! How! How!" It became a contest of *'How versus Holy, and for now, the How's were winning!'* The confusion swirled into a canopy of blackness making it seem that some of the stars in Rakia hid their light not in fear, but in shame. Leviathan joined in the contest clamoring, "As Satan has questioned, why? Satan asks why and we should too. Now, every one of you shouts why! Why should Elyon be named our God?"

The piercing white of ♎ Satan's squinty eyes peering out of the thick black mist made for a scene that shook the confidence of the most courageous among the angels. In the distance, the immensely bright beacon of Elyon's Throne beckoned, sending shafts of *'Light Trails'* into the darkness to lead the *'worried warriors'* away from danger.

The Prodigal Satan

CHAPTER FOUR
LOVERS OF DARKNESS

John 3:19 - "And this is the condemnation, that light is come into the world, and men loved darkness rather than light, because their deeds were evil."

Those who returned to the light did so in fear of the encroaching darkness, but those who remained behind in the black mist were beguiled by the experience, became mesmerized and motionless. Yet, another angel of influence named Belial[1] rose up to rant, ♎ red eyes sparkling like amber stars setting over the horizon of Rahab.[2] "Satan will be our god, ♎ taunted. ♎ has created something greater than Elyon ever did. Satan's words are true and proven by the sign and wonder ♎ created. Darkness is greater than light. It brings freedom to every creature. Elyon segregated and suppressed us, using ♍ light to expose us, robbing us of our individuality. Satan's murky mist that conceals us allows freedom of expression and covers us from the spying of *'Elyon's multi-eyed Ophanim.'* "We have been set free to speak great things even against the so called Most High."

Satan applauded the speech of Belial, which was so effective, vilifying the venerated Elyon and the Ophanim.

Belial would be valuable in the coming revolt. "Belial, no one but me has ever spoken as eloquently as you just did. You surely are with me, by my side forever. I am The Satan, you are my oracle."

Belial was overwhelmed, "I owe it all to you Satan. You were not afraid to speak out against Elyon, and behold the beauty of the blackness you created! Outside of darkness, I

1 Belial - Angel of Counsel - The name means "Useless." Useless counsel.

2 The ancient abode of Satan.

was cowardly and quiet. You have given me voice. You god deserve the glory!"

What appeared as an ominous cloud to some, served as a concealing cloak for the crimes of the *"Crooks of the Cosmos."* Covertly, the coming of *'dark angels'* had crept in. The *'Lovers of Light'* shiningly stood out in stark contrast to the demons that disregarded their inherent, God like *'goodness nature.'* Going forward, Satan lusts for nothing short of the absolute destruction light, achieving the domination of darkness!

CHAPTER FIVE
MERCY OR MAHEYM

It was a monumental meeting without precedent, truly *apocalyptic in nature. ♈ was first to address the august body of beings in attendance. He began speaking with a voice that sounded like the rushing of many waters,*[1] *and his eyes burning like a thousand suns. Yet His message was clear, deliberate and distinct, "Gabriel, Michael, Raphael, Uriel, Raguel, Ramiel, Saraquel, You have heard my voice, known my thoughts, but have never spoken to Me. Something happened that has changed My heavens forever, yet you come at my bidding, as others led by Satan rise up in revolt." There was a pause that seemingly invited a response. Gabriel raised ♎ mighty voice but it quivered with timidity as ♎ words to ♈ were a first for any to directly address the Almighty. Your Holiness," ♎ eked out, "nothing is hidden from your sight, but we, your servants discovered that Satan has incited an insurrection among many of the Malakim. We have no way of knowing how or where this ends, but You, Holy One know all things."*

♈ shook the heavens with ♍ response, "You Gabriel, like your peers, Satan, Beelzebub, Leviathan and all the angels, are as I made you, with will and freedom of choice. You are created for my pleasure, not to protest and cause pandemonium.

Gabriel felt a fiery dart go through ♎ at being called *'a Peer of the Prince of Perdition.'*

Bene Elyon wasn't finished, "Let Satan roar and revolt,

1 Revelation 1:15, Revelation 19:6, Revelation 14:2, Ezekiel 43:2 - "And, behold, the glory of the God of Israel came from the way of the east: and his voice was like a noise of many waters: and the earth shined with his glory."

or you Gabriel, Michael, any of you; there will be no other gods beside me.[1] Only your allegiance attested to by your attendance here in My presence has prevailed upon Me not to *'destroy'*[2] you, along with the treasonous ones."

Panic struck the repenting Malakim as they watched their leaders the archangels first fall back and then go prostrate before ♈. The most powerful of all the archangels, Michael felt ♎ strength wane in the presence of the One who possessed such authority. "Holy One, we don't know or understand the word, *'destroy.'* "It sounds and seems so fearful," ♎ added. A long pause ensued and Michael awkwardly requested, "Is it the opposite of creation, the wonderful way you created us?"

Another long pause ensued. Every angel trembled in fear that silence might signal the start of the dreaded *'destroy.'*

Ramiel did not wait for an answer that none of the angels wanted to hear. ♎ was aware that ♎ appeal for Mercy must be made at once. Bowing before ♈, with ♎ crimson colored body turning a deeper red, Ramiel, worried that ♎ words would fail. He solemnly pled, "Most Magnificent and Holy One, permit me to state our cause. We have come into your presence with shocked sensibilities concerning the sedition of Satan. As You do know all things, it is needless for me to inform You of anything. None of us kneeling here in Your presence were privy to the devious plans of Satan. We will never agree with nor make an alliance with Satan or any of ♎ emissaries. Cast them away if you will, but we remain loyal to You and You only. We exist only to do Your will and stand ever ready to resist any revolt against You. Tell us what *'destroy'* is and if You endow us with the power, we will destroy

1 Deuteronomy 32:39 - "See now that I myself am he! There is no god besides me."

2 Destroy their bodies only. Their Spirits are eternal.

those who defy You!"

Bene Elyon was silent. ♍ had never destroyed anything. Would ♍ destroy something ♍ had called *'Good?'* The angels gaped in utter astonishment as the entirety of The Throne turned a deep shade of red, matching the compassionate color of Ramiel. A ruby red fluid gushed from its base washing over them all, including the garments[1] of Bene Elyon! Gazing upon Ramiel's color, they sensed that Mercy was granted. Now they truly knew the meaning of *'Holy'* and had no fear of the yet unknown *'destroy.'* The Chayot led out in rapturous singing!!!

1 Isaiah 63:1 - "Who is this coming from Edom, from Bozrah, with his garments stained crimson?"

CHAPTER SIX
A SECOND OPINION

The unholy alliance huddled closely to conspire for their coup. They were about to have their confidence compromised even as their conceit reached its crest!

Satan cackled, “Did you see them run away? I have achieved the ultimate victory by creating darkness. It will be our weapon with which we will take down Elyon’s false hierarchy of holiness. Yes, we will destroy the illusion of light using our darkness. Imagine, Uriel, Gabriel, and Michael, all of them afraid of the dark, afraid of me. I became their god, their lord at the moment that they turned and fled. This is how I know the Elyon is not God; I have no fear of him,” Satan countered by exuding confidence hoping to calm and cajole ♎ followers.

Beelzebub and Leviathan motioned with their hands and the remaining rebel Malakim went wild with approbation and applause!

Without notice or warning a light brighter than one thousand suns rushed toward them, interrupting their premature celebration.

The dark mist that hung heavy over the meeting shattered into millions of pieces of shiny slivers of light beams as Michael, supercharged from being in the presence of Bene Elyon, swooped down into their midst. Every demon suddenly felt uncovered, endangered and exposed in the presence of the most powerful angel in Elyon’s arsenal.

Michael offered no excuse for interrupting, nor did ♎ parse words with platitudes. “You are gathered here illegally against The Most High God. You have deceived yourselves into doubting that ♍ knows everything. ♍ sees you right now, even as you cower before me and I am not at all His equal. It is only because ♍ called you Good that you still exist. You Satan have never heard of the word *'destroy,'* but ♈ told me its meaning and it is so terrifying I cannot describe it. You rebels have put all of the angels all in peril and I have come to persuade you to turn from your evil plan. Otherwise, I will petition Elyon for permission to deploy *'destroy'* and I will bring it down upon you myself."

Satan was speechless! As Michael took leave, Leviathan was found hiding behind Beelzebub. A haunting hush stilled the heavens with a silence louder than the sound of Satan's *'deafening disobedience.'*

Abaddon,[1] one of Beelzebub's captains, spoke up with a quivering bravado born out of sheer terror of Michael. "Satan, we have no choice but to heed the words of Michael. ♎ openly challenged us with ♎ display of power, the likes of which we have never seen. Do any of us have the strength to defeat ♎? If indeed we are found out, it may be too late, but we have heard of Mercy being attributed to God. The word Mercy is inscribed on the sides of Elyon's Throne."

A serpentine Seraphim named Pythus[2] weighed in with a voice much calmer than that of Abaddon, "I don't know where we might escape to or if we can even evade Elyon, if indeed ♍ is omnipresent, but as for me, I choose to chance leaving. May I suggest, as I explored the heavenly quadrants, way beyond where the beautiful Piscesian planet Rahab[3] revolves, I beheld many other pleasant places that we can conquer and inhabit."

"Since we are opposed to Elyon and ♍ kingdom,

1 Abaddon - A captain of the Host known for great strength.

2 Pythus - The Python - A Seraphim chosen by Satan to tell and perpetrate lies.

3 Psalms 89:10 - speaks of Rahab! The Planet Elyon destroyed. Located between Mars and Jupiter. The remains are the asteroid belt that circles between the two planets.

perhaps ♍ would be glad to be rid of us and give us Rahab as our own kingdom."

Abaddon agreed, "I detest being dominated. Perhaps we can take advantage of Elyon's so called Mercy and convince ♍ that ♍ is better off without us. We will do ♍ a favor. Michael told us that ♈ is reluctant to speak of this word *'destroy.'* With my plan, ♍ will not have to *'destroy'* anything."

Pythus was anxious, "I must say, what a *'brilliantly dark'*[1] plan you propose! We will say that given Mercy, we will reform and return to do ♍ service."

Satan, was prepared to accept the plan of action, when the lovely angel Lilith,[2] second in beauty only to Satan and never far from ♎ side, seductively and secretively whispered in ♎ ear.

"You should steal these words to be your own."

Satan warmed to these words of wisdom. It didn't take long for ♎ devious mind to devise a plan that could accomplish both escaping from Elyon and grabbing the greatest gift in all the Universe.

♎ concluded, "Aha, my fellows, you are wise to have suggested the exact plan that I expected to submit to you for my enactment."

"Let me explain," Satan continued with a hint of distain in ♎ voice, "You will see when I return from beguiling our *'Big Brother,'* my plan is greater that you can imagine. Wait, watch and wonder at Me, Darkness and Deceit will reign supreme!"

1 Oxymoron - a figure of speech that combines contradictory terms. Typical of the way demons talk with intention to cause confusion.

2 Lilith - Jewish mythology - a goat like angel with long hair -a demon that screeches by night in the desert. Isaiah 34:14 - "The wild beasts of the desert shall also meet with the wild beasts of the island, and the satyr shall cry to his fellow; the 'screech owl' (Lilith) also shall rest there, and find for herself a place of rest."

The Prodigal Satan

CHAPTER SEVEN
STOLEN PROPERTY

Psalms 24:1 - "The earth is the Lord's, and the fullness thereof; the world, and they that dwell therein."

One of the inscriptions on the side of the Throne went something like this, "You shall not desire that which belongs to another." This saying always annoyed Satan.

Satan realized that ♎ should not approach or appear anywhere around the Throne adorned in ♎ recently donned dark dress uniform. With a shudder that shook ♎ soldiers standing nearby, ♎ unsuccessfully cast off ♎ shroud of darkness as ♎ strained to regain his shine. "I am going to claim what is mine. What is ours," ♎ quickly corrected.

Beelzebub and Leviathan gave each other a questioning glance, smirking as Satan caught the slip of ♎ forked tongue. Satan dared not hesitate long enough to take a breath, being alert that ♎ audience managed to catch on to ♎ canard!

"Do I understand what you are saying Satan? You are going to ask..."

Satan defiantly interrupted, "Ask you say? Ask? I will ask for nothing Leviathan. I know what is ours and I will demand nothing less. I have conferred with Pythus who is over the southern bottle of Pisces.[1]

Once while *'wandering,'* ♎ happened upon what may hold the supreme secret of ♈. It is a place called Earth and it is most desirable of all the stones, at least the ones that Pythus has seen."

"What? What about this place? Where is it and what is it," Beelzebub inquired.

Satan deceptively replied, "At the center."

1 Pisces - The constellation of the serpent.

Not wishing to seem uninformed, all in attendance nodded as though they knew what and where the center was, but such was not the case.

“Pythus told me of a strange sight on Earth and I had to see for myself. We dared not trespass there, but touching the stone was not necessary for me to become intrigued. From above, I beheld a strange shaped object and the glare of it shot up toward us like a fiery flash off of the surface of this brilliant blue stone called Earth. Pythus and I are certain there is a coded message contained in this special structure.”

Satan fluently fibbed, “It is a message that can only be known by ♈ and I. See, I am now His equal. Who ever controls the stones will control the heavens also. Then *‘I will’* be ♈ god! This is our destiny and *‘I will’* seize it for us from this Son of Elyon.”

Satan did not yet know the code, but was convinced that the strange shaped structure would contain the answer to ♎ questions. “Who knows, perhaps Elyon’s key to knowledge is deposited there,” ♎ mused! “I am determined not be denied what I know to be ♎ destiny.”

Pythus was quickly becoming Satan’s confidant much to the chagrin of Lilith. Satan was not inclined to listen to many others, unless of course it served ♎ purposes.

Pythus politely pled, “Satan, your deep dark color is a thing to be desired for those of us that revere you, but I fear that it will be offensive to ♈ and lessen our chance of deceiving Him.”

Satan snarled but subdued ♎ skepticism long enough to hear what Pythus, *‘the master of misinformation’* might have to say.

Pythus continued, “Please understand, there is no doubt that you are exquisite just as you are, excluding what Elyon might expect or accept. Being of the order of the Seraphim, I still possess part of my *'pyrotechnic potency.'* I can somewhat illuminate on demand. Let me approach ♈ as though I remain in the light. I would only do this for you, for us. I will convince ♍ of our intent to reform, if only granted the gift of ♍ Grace and given the prize of allowing us to possess the Earth."

Satan warmed to the words of the fiery Seraphim, but the heat of Pythus' discourse did nothing to change Satan's darkened coloration.

"I will convince ♈ that we are ♍ servants..."

This made *'the heinous hell raiser'* growl, "Servants?"

"Please, please allow me," Pythus implored, "I will mislead ♍ that we as servants will tend ♍ gardens, guard ♍ treasures and cause the Earth to flourish. Elyon will happily allow us to take our Imps[1] with us to inhabit and eventually inherit the Earth. If Bene Elyon is so godlike, ♍ does not need our worship. ♍ can create others who will blindly bless ♍ Holiness! We will never again be servants to any. We will be our own Elyon!"

Satan's snarl uncurled into a sneering smile as ♎ dreamed of deceiving the deity that so disquieted ♎! Lilith embraced Satan as ♎ gently wrapped ♎ long straight red locks of hair around Satan's face and neck soothing ♎.

1 A small demon

CHAPTER EIGHT
GRAPPLING[1] WITH GRACE

Charles J. Rolls[2] wrote, "The riches of His Grace are reckon-less in spiritual blessings...The riches of His Goodness are numberless...The riches of His Wisdom are measureless, as demonstrated in the plan and purpose of salvation, redemption, reconciliation and regeneration...The riches of His glory are traceless in that they are ageless, ceaseless and changeless..."

Pythus approached the Throne carefully, intimidated by it's inscriptions now highlighted by the change in color to a crimson shade. "Elyon, I come here to ask..."

Elyon abruptly interrupted, "I know".

"You have yet to hear..."

"I know," Elyon demanded

"Who has informed..."

"I know. Pythus, I have no need of any information from you or any other. I not only know the question, I am the answer. I also know the deceit deposited in you by the devil and I know you are here dishonestly thinking you can deceive me concerning your devices. I am aware of the deceptiveness of your yet unspoken demands."

Pythus' lips moved but no words came, just a stammering stutter of stupefaction.

Elyon sternly rebuked Pythus, "Fortunately for you, Satan and the rest of ♎ rebellious renegades, the conviction of conscience that I created in you, makes change possible. Unfortunately, you have the prerogative to pursue plans other

1 Grapple - A contest for superiority.

2 Dr. Charles J. Rolls - The great Religious rhyme maker, wrote a series of 5 books on the names and titles of Christ!

than those I designed and desired for you." Pythus finally regained enough composure to mutter, "But what if you are mistaken?"

"Pythus, you will learn, but your lesson will be lasting, even everlasting. I will grant your greediness by giving my Grace to you without your gratitude or gratefulness."

"Why would you if you really know?" Pythus queried.

"Your question itself condemns you Pythus. Go your way now, you and all who have conspired with you. Go and enthrone Satan on Earth, but I give you this warning. Do not harm the Earth. Change yourself if you will, but be careful not to change the earth. The Earth was created by and for ♈ and ♈ made it exactly the way that ♈ desired. It belongs to the Firstborn and His Faithful, the Meek, not Madmen, the Humble, not the Haughty such as you and Satan. I warn you a second time, as a true witness of my oath. I will destroy you if the Earth is degraded, damaged or destroyed[1] in any way, by any demon!"

1 Revelation 11:18 - "The time has come to destroy those who have destroyed the Earth."

The Prodigal Satan

CHAPTER NINE
GAMMONED[1] BY GRACE

From Milton's Paradise Lost Part two, 18 "Heaven's law made me your leader. The rights of justice gave us free will. And our achievements gave us honor and glory. 22 Now we have it all back again, and in a much safer place. He willingly gave us this kingdom. Nobody would want to take it away from us. 35 That makes us more firmly united. Now we can fight for what is rightly ours. 39 We have a better chance of succeeding now than when we were in the comforts of Heaven."

Pythus was beside ♎self with gammoned glee at the prospect of presenting a misguided message from Elyon to the Evil One. "I did it, Satan, I..."

Satan snapped, "You did it? Do you dare to demand credit for my creativity. You did nothing but what I warranted you to do."

Pythus politely prostrated ♎self before the pious Prince of darkness. "Please forgive me. I sadly succumbed to the sublimity of our success. You should know by now that my loyalty to your lordship has no limits."

"There you go again, telling me what I should know, Pythus."

Pythus sensed that it was time for ♎ to snake ♎ way out of this conversation. "You have prevailed O' Prince of Perdition. Now let ♈ make His claims, or even Elyon, whoever they are. I can't tell, god, gods, angels, but whatever their Godhead is, there is room for you my Satan!"

Satan grinned a ghoulish smirk and loudly sighed with ghastly satisfaction.

1 Gammoned means Deceived.

The Prodigal Satan

Pythus was cheered and continued, "So much for omniscience. If ♍ really comprehended our conniving, there is no way ♍ would agree to our acquiring or even accessing the Earth. We must move hastily before ♍ hears of or fathoms the fakery that we are formulating."

"You are so right, Pythus. Once we inherit, or as ♈ would say, inhabit the Earth, there will be no stopping us. The strange shaped stone on Earth contains the secrets of the Sons of god and we will use them to defeat and topple the tyrannical self-proclaimed totalitarian deity Elyon."

"There is nothing covert or confidential that ♍ can conceal from us. Knowledge is ♍ power and we will acquire and annex Earth as a sub-kingdom to Rahab. Once we procure it, we will have prevailed over ♍. Rahab, the Earth, then the Universes!"

The two diabolical *'demon-strators'* hurried off into the depths of darkness to declare victory to untold numbers of awaiting angels, victims of the *'venomous viper's fabrications.'* Conceit converted angels into, fallen, faithless, derelict demons, disdainful of truth. *'Pride is the highest pedestal from which any can fall!' It is destructive; its disciples are soon defeated by self-deception, its followers foiled by vain flattery of their selves!*[1]

1 Proverbs 16:18 "- Pride precedes a disaster, and an arrogant attitude precedes a fall."

CHAPTER TEN
RENDEZVOUS ON RAHAB

1st John 3:8 - "He who is doing the sin, of the devil he is, because from the beginning the devil doth sin; for this was the Son of God manifested, that he may break up the works of the devil."

The watery Piscesian Planet Rahab, abode of Satan was abuzz with angels arriving from every bottle of heaven at the bequest of Satan. The Beautiful One's plan threatening the tranquility of Elyon's kingdom was trending toward triumph.

Myriads of misguided messengers furiously flew toward a future damming them to demon-hood. They came at the call couriered to them by fiery fiends[1] loyal to Satan. Though staunch supporters, they would soon be Satan's slaves. Satan's quest was a colossal undertaking, intended to conquer and control nothing less than everything that belonged to Bene Elyon.

Chosen to command the masses were Abaddon, Beelzebub, Belial, Leviathan, Mammon and Pythus. There was some semblance of Satan in each of these six select soldiers. Satan barked his orders, "Abaddon, you are called to choose those among us who are apt to use force in our fight to overthrow the onerous One who opts to own us."

"You can certainly count on my commitment to combat any that comes against you, my Satan."

"Belial, it will be your responsibility to report to me concerning the cerebral condition of our comrades. It is imperative that we all believe in our cause and that none waver in the coming conflict. Pride and ego are the banners of

1 Fiend - A mean or evil one.

our confederacy as we go into combat." Satan solicited a war before one even started.

Belial had always fancied the favor of Satan by heaping flattery on ♎. "Your confidence in our cause will keep us composed and conceited. With you as our Commander, causalities nor calamities can ever come our way."

Satan preened! "Well said, Belial. Only I could have said it better." Without waiting for a snide remark, ♎ abruptly raised ♎ voice to a feverish shrill tone, intending to incite passion.

"Beelzebub, I am heavily relying on you to rile up the angels, keeping their resistance at a riotous pitch. Use every dirty tactic to discredit any stubborn angels who resist our revolt."

"I am with you now as I was at the start," Beelzebub vowed. You know me well, considering my talents are suited for subversion. ♎ spoke slowly touching and bumping all twelve of ♎ spiny fingers together in a show of confidence. "My ability to make convincing arguments is more than adequate. I will not fail you."

Satan bordered on a serious jest, "I agree that you are adroit at arguing Beelzebub. Often it seems that you dare to contradict me."

This made Beelzebub feel awkward, but yet ♎ experienced a sense of empowerment, upon hearing ♎ irritated Satan in such a way.

"You Leviathan, the great and terrible Monster of the miry deep; what a great role you will play. I first saw you as you rose from the waves of water, my sea serpent. I praise the swells that swept you ashore, here on Rahab. Your assignment is vital to our success. We must convince the angels that Elyon did not create them. Boast that ♍ claims are bogus. I also call on you to devise a deceitful doctrine. Declare that all we creatures, great and small are descendants from the depths of the oceans. Tell that the waters are much too deep and devoid of light for Elyon, who claims to be Light, to have formed any of us. We are truly Children of darkness. *There is no creator God, we are creatures of chance; angelic accidents!"*

"Fire came boiling from the mouth and nostrils of Leviathan as ♎ was being honored in such fashion by Satan.

"You Leviathan, will legitimize the lie that none of us came from a creator. Water is the womb that birthed everything, just as it did you my blessed behemoth!"

"You are wise to choose me for this task; it will not only be my doctrine that brings us success. There is none other like me in length or height, size and strength. I will subdue every creature that swims in the sea and control everything that creeps or crawls on the ground. Everything I do will be for your glory only!"

Satan squirmed at the braggadocios statement of Leviathan and was about to spout off when Pythus, *'the maestro of misrepresentation'* headed off trouble. "What a wonderful combination for confusion; Leviathan coming from liquid. We will call it evolution. *Plankton*[1] *evolves into the Platypus,*[2] *The tadpole becomes the Tyrannosaurs, from a germ to a giant, water to a wallaby,*[3] *liquid to Leviathan.* Not one angel will remain that believes they came from a creator."

Satan's anger was somewhat assuaged and ♎ let *'Leviathan off the hook,'*[4] with one insincere word, "Perfect."

The irony of *'imperfection'* using the word *'perfect.'*

1 Plankton is the base of marine ecosystems, providing food for larger animals.

2 Platypus has a duck like snout, short legs, webbed feet, and a beaver tail.

3 A semi-aquatic mammal.

4 Author's pun intended.

The Prodigal Satan

"Mammon, being as you have mastered the mining of minerals and are aware of their potential purchasing power, I pronounce you the Prince of pricing, procurement, buying and bartering. You will assist me in accumulating the assets needed to advance our authoritarian administration. If necessary we will steal or use stealth to secure our Kingdom."

"But Satan, Rahab's roads are paved with gold. Its avenues are accessible via silver walkways. Your abode is adorned with the most common of all the minerals and metals found here in your home territory. How can we make goods as common as gold, silver and platinum valuable?"

Satan stood looking stunned, "You are wise in the area of storing wealth Mammon, but your ignorance of obtaining it illustrates why you need me. I know that the concept of obtaining and owning is unknown to you, in that ♈ controls everything in ♈ Kingdom, where we could neither claim nor possess anything. It all belongs to ♈. With us, it will be a matter of supply and demand.

"Supply and what? I don't understand demand."

"I know, we have never been able to demand anything, but now, *'I will.'* We will hoard and hide the heavy metals, make them hard to find. Rarity makes for rapacity,[1] scarcity for surfeiting.[2] We will create classes and cultures. We will use the slyness of our system to subjugate others into servitude to us. By controlling the wealth, we can control the worlds."

Beelzebub looked inquisitively at Leviathan, "Classes he said? Servants? Isn't that what we are supposedly revolting against Leviathan?" Leviathan shook ♎ gnarly head in disbelief and distrust.

Mammon was oblivious, "I understand quite well my lord and I will never forget the lesson of lucre that I just

1 Intense selfish desire for wealth.

2 Going beyond what is usual or proper.

learned from you."

"Listen to me," Satan!

"Pythus, I have saved my instructions to you for last. You stand next to me as my mouthpiece. Your words are beautiful, like Leviathan's body.

They twist in serpentine fashion to form a tapestry, threaded together with truth and untruth. This serves our tangled purposes so well. You are *'my preacher, my purveyor of perversion, my speaker of sinister sayings, my litigator of lies, my trash talker'*."

"I only repeat the words I learn from you, my menacing mentor. You are the founding Father of lies and liars. I have learned to speak in your native language.[1] My speech is your slave and it my tongue will serve whenever you summon."

Satan was flattered by the title Father.

Pythus added, "I will make cursing commonplace, accompanied by useless arguments, fighting, fussing, hurtful and hateful words. This will serve as subterfuge to keep others distracted from our strategy and our scheme secret and secure."

Satan wanted no one to understand or misunderstand what a lie is. To understand lying makes it willful and with Satan it needs to be natural. To misunderstand it would affect its effect. "It longs to be magical and mystical, entertaining, embellishing and enslaving."

♎ reasoned, "My lying is an act of creation. I take nothing more than my thoughts, my fantasies, and reason them to be reality, just like Elyon claims ♍ Logos did. How am I not like Logos?"

The forked tongued one summed it up by saying; "A lie is not evil in and of itself, just as evil serves its purpose.

1 John 8:44 - "You belong to your father the devil...When he lies, he speaks his native language, for he is a liar and the father of lies."

The Prodigal Satan

We are not evil because we reject Elyon. Elyon is the true tyrant, even if ♍ proved to be the creator. Consider the cruel and unusual punishment of being compelled to perpetually praise anything. *'Holy without ceasing, adoration without rest, applause without recess, approbation without repose.'* Arrggggg, I have had it with unwillful worship."

Beelzebub, the troublemaker could not suppress the thought, "Satan hates worship, unless it is directed to ♎." Luckily for Beelzebub, Satan did not have access to ♎ thoughts.

Satan decided every demon was in place for the *'success of the succession.'* It was time to make the big move.

The Prodigal Satan

CHAPTER ELEVEN
THE CRIMSON CORDED CULPRIT

In ancient Greece a criminal (the pharmakos-sorcerer) was cast out of the community, either in response to a natural disaster or in response to a calendrical crisis (such as the end of the year). In the Bible, the scapegoat was a goat that was designated Azazel to be outcast in the desert as part of the ceremonies of the Day of Atonement.

The scene looked like what we Humanoids would identify as a massive meteor shower accompanied by asteroids and comets, but in reality it was searing streaks of demons descending to the terra firma of Earth. Leading the way in the furious fall was the *'Son of the Morning'*[1] Satan, adorned like an angelic astronaut for the occasion of occupying ♎ new outpost. Satan was easily recognized, for the strangest thing happened as ♎ began the journey to Earth. As ♎ lifted up from Rahab, ♈ appeared in the atmosphere, aggressively

1 Isaiah 14:12 - "How you have fallen from heaven, morning star, son of the dawn!" The earliness of Satan's title of 'morning star' supports the idea that ♎ was created near or second to ♈.

approaching ♎. ♈ wore a crimson colored cord as a cincture[1] around ♈ clothing. Needless to say, the shock of the sudden arrival of an unexpected adversary caused much unholy anxiety in Satan.

"Whaattt, Bene Elyon, whaattt is the purpose of your, your, your coming here?" Satan stammered.

Satan was fearful ♈ would alter the arrangement agreed to between ♎self and Elyon.

"Who am I dealing with? I asked them both who they are and they say, 'I Am." ♎ could not comprehend the uncomplicated Godhead; that there is no separation, schism or split in the Oneness of God.[2]

♈ responded, "I didn't come here. I was and I Am here. There is nowhere that you can flee from my presence. When you arrive at your there or your here, I am present."

This had Satan's mind spinning. In a moment of self-doubt, ♎ pondered, "Perhaps, I am not His equal."

"Stay calm Satan, I am here to give you what you unjustly believe you deserve. You cowardly sent Pythus to ask for the Earth and now I bequeath it to you. You will reign as king over My estate the Earth, but the upper heavens that surround it will remain under My supervision. I bestow upon you the title, '*Prince of the air,*'[3] but as such, there will be parameters to your power."

Satan didn't want to make known ♎ real motives, so ♎ swallowed hard and remained silent. Again thinking, "Who is ♈ to preside over my powers."

1 A cord or sash of cloth worn around an ecclesiastical vestment or the habit of a religious person.

2 Romans 1:20 - "For his invisible attributes, namely, his eternal power and divine nature, have been clearly perceived, ever since the creation of the world, in the things that have been made. So they are without excuse."

3 Ephesians 2:2 - "Prince and power of the air."

The Prodigal Satan

♈ wasn't finished, "I know that you wish to usurp my planet and undermine my plans, yet I am willing to grant you grace."

"Pythus made our plans plain to any who were willing to trust in our truthfulness or value our veracity," Satan explained.

"It is hard to trust a '*truant*'[4] like you. You were assigned to the brightest and blessed planet Rahab, but now you desert like it is a barren desert. You were allowed to cover the coveted altar, but now you despise it. You were authorized to make music and perpetually lead praise, yet now you deplore it. You were allowed to be next to me, but now you detest the very thought of it."

Satan was shaken at the thought of being found out and longed for darkness to cover ♎.

Left speechless, ♎ managed to scream, "Pythus, get here now." Pythus stood still, mute and paralyzed, hiding among the horde of disabled demons.

Pythus had promised to speak for Satan, but there was nothing to say. Only to wonder, "What will Satan do with me if ♎ survives? What will happen to me if ♎ doesn't survive?"

For now, Satan the deserter knew what it felt like to be deserted.

Heaven fell silent in anticipation of what would happen next. Not even one Holy, Holy, Holy was heard.

♈ slowly began unwrapping the blood colored cord from around His own garment.

"This red rope is the symbol of my rights as firstborn of all creation and I am placing it on you. Go now and make your choices and allow My grace to grow as gratitude in your ungrateful spirit. The color of this cord is a mystery and its meaning is known only by Me. The riddle will be revealed

4 One who shirks their duty.

when all things are made ready. If you repent of your rebellion and truly reform, the color of this cord will turn white. All of heaven will be waiting, watching and wanting the cord and you to change as well."

No reply or retort was forthcoming from Satan or Pythus. This was not a conversation. It was a lecture. "Further, I am assigning another name for you. On Earth, you will be addressed as '*Azazel.'*[1]

This name "Goat" identifies you as a Capricorn,[2] based upon the bottle of heaven from whence you came. Azazel the "Goat" created for greatness. This future can still be yours, but you must renounce your ways and repent. You, the one with the red rope for a robe; the sedition and sin of every angel that follows after you will be upon your head. They will rise and fall with you.

You will either ascend to the heights of Zevul once again, or be cast into *'the crematorium at the core and center of the Earth'* that you so crave. Satan was shaken by serious-

1 Azazel is an alias of Satan which identifies d as a goat. The Name means "One sent away."

2 The Satanic Pentagram contains the name Leviathan. Its center is a goat's head the goat being the symbol of Capricorn.

ness of the *'sentencing'* from the Savior that ♎ so despised.

"You can go now. I release you to either *'reform or radicalize'* yourself. Remember, I will destroy those who damage, debase or do anything detrimental to the Earth.

Azazel flew so fast that ♎ protesting partners could hardly keep pace even as they entered a *'worm hole'*[1] which propelled them to Earth at a speed faster than light, providing them a much needed journey in the blackout. Their dark spirits basked in the feeling of being hidden from ♈. "What is this crimson cord about?" was Azazel's first question upon arrival.

Pythus, *'Satan's spin doctor,'* adroitly attempted to make ♈ words sound favorable.

"♈ surrendered to you. Don't trust ♈ threats. They are idle and impotent. Look at yourself. You now wear *'the sash of superiority.'* ♈ bestowing this red rope on you is ♈ admission that you came before ♈. You are first of all creatures, Son of the Dawn! If ♈ is a god, then you are God of gods. Wear it proudly. It is your *'Sash of Superiority'.*"

The red rope indeed was a *'fetter of favor'* but Azazel did not consider it as such, and named it, *'Bene Elyon's constraining chain.'*

1 A shortcut through "space time." $(\partial\Sigma \sim S2)=\Omega$

CHAPTER TWELVE
FROM EMPYREAN[1] TO ELYSIAN FIELDS[2]

[3]

Azazel was overwhelmed with excitement as ♎ watched myriads of militant mercenaries descend from the worm hole onto planet Earth. Together, they stood looking back at distant stationary star named 'Sol.' It was too far flung to provide bright light to earth, but close enough to keep a constant twilight in place, which absolutely irritated Azazel.

Azazel interrupted the solitude of staring at Sol, "No more time for star gazing, so get busy!"

♎ Generals eagerly evaluated each regimen of renegade angels as they arrived. They were segregated according to their particular abilities. Abaddon, Beelzebub, Belial,

1 Empyrean is used as a name for the firmament and in Christian literature for the dwelling-place of God.

2 A place of admission reserved for mortals related to the gods and other heroes to live out their existence in bliss.

3 Camille Flammarion's L'atmosphere.

The Prodigal Satan

Leviathan, Mammon, Pythus; all lined up to enlist the soldiers of Satan into d service.

"Fall in. Over here, they yelled!" The Malakim were prone to meandering around, wide-eyed at where they were.

In a frenzy they asked one another, "Who are you? What are you and where do we go?"

The confusion continued, "Laborers, over here, liars over there. Workers fall in, warriors fall out." So many terms that the angels were not familiar with. None of this made any sense, compared to the simplicity of being known as *'Worshipers'* where the just came from!

Belial the dealmaker tried advising, "Lord Azazel, why don't you give the Malakim a little time to acclimate, being as all they are accustomed to is worship? Why the need for such militancy?"

Azazel, was the recipient of *'the greatest gift ever bestowed on bad behavior.'* ♎ stubbornly settled on a path to squander it.

The advice had absolutely no affect, "Mammon, start your excavations immediately. Do not leave one stone unturned. Gather and garner every metal, mineral or stone of value and bring it to our ♎ storehouse. Leviathan, take to the water. Make a record of every *'kind'* that swims or subsists therein. Survey the land listing every species, making sure of our safety reporting any dangerous sort to Abaddon."

"Abaddon, quickly find the most ferocious of the fiery ones among us. Take them and secure this planet against any possible enemies that ♈ may have planted here!"

"Beelzebub, round up all that remain behind for a massive rally. Pythus will prepare the speeches. It is imperative that we inspire these imps if we are to ask them for the perspiration of their brow."

"Belial, you will assist me in establishing a society of

secrecy. I expect you to report directly to me any seditious or subversive sentence spoken on Earth."

"Maybe, just maybe it's not so easy for every demon to be a devil." 'The kingdom Azazel promised was not to be the kingdom produced.' Azazel's true nature was that of a Pharaoh, *'plundering the earth, pirating its wealth and punishing its population.'*

Abaddon religiously trained ♎ troops, but for no rational reason. After many forays to the four corners of Earth, ♎ found not even one enemy, natural or supernatural. Although, ♎ did report the presence of many species of land animals and all sorts of flying creatures. They posed no threat to Abaddon and seemed not to notice ♎ or the horde of troops.

"Azazel, my report to you is that an army is unnecessary as it pertains to this planet. I worry for Leviathan, for there is little seawater here. Earth is mostly land and more land. There are no mountains and valleys observable here as on some of other stones. There are few places for anyone to hide, unless it is among the trees or here in the thick vegetation."

"Abaddon, we will keep the forces ready to fight. Understood? I have enemies that you are yet to envision and epic battles to engage in that you can't begin to imagine."

This confused Abaddon, "If I am the commander, why the lack of confidence? Why would you not feel comfortable to confide in me?"

"Abaddon, stay calm. Your conduct is unbecoming of one who would be confident commander. I will hold nothing back from you when collaboration is called for. As I said, you gave a good report, especially concerning the Earth's land mass. The more mass, the more minerals and metals are here for us to harvest. Have you told Mammon yet?"

Satan's selfish side was showing!

Sarcastically, Abaddon shot back, "No, I would not for all this earth deprive you of the joy of informing Mammon that you care to collaborate with ♎ about uncovering your cherished cache of treasures."

The noise of Leviathan lumbering through the lushness of Elysian Fields interrupted the impending incident between Azazel and Abaddon. Leviathan moved slowly enjoying the dew that descended daily on the vegetation, as it dampened d drying scaly body. Though amphibious[1], ♎ seemed to prefer the sea to the soil.

Azazel noticed, "Seeing you are back from searching the sea so soon, you must not have found anything there to threaten us."

"I beheld some wondrous sights in the depths. There were whales, serpents, seals, swimmers of every size and shape submerged in the sea. All was tranquil in the deep. We could consider moving our entire kingdom there if all of you were just like me!"

Azazel felt fury rise up, hearing Leviathan being so brazen as to suggest that everyone be like ♎.

"You braggadocios behemoth; why would you possibly propose we all look or live like you Leviathan?"

"It's not that, it's... it's...just... that...I...I...I rule there...," Leviathan stuttered.

Things quickly went from bad to worse.

"Now you are crossing the line. You want us to be like you and come under your rule."

Leviathan swung away so violently that his posterior appendage nearly bashed Belial, Beelzebub and other bystanders.

If the truth were told, there was trouble in "Paradise." The world of demons is not a peaceful place. It is a kingdom

1 Capable of living on land and in water.

of chaos, confusion and confrontation commingled with weeping, wailing, groaning and gnashing of teeth.[1] This is their nature, for *God is not the one who wrote the handbook on confusion.*[2]

1 Matthew 13:42 - "In that place there will be weeping and gnashing of teeth. And they (The Angels) shall cast them into a furnace of fire: there shall be wailing and gnashing of teeth."

2 1st Corinthians 14:33 - "For God is not the author of confusion but of peace..."

CHAPTER THIRTEEN
FROM THE THRONE TO THE TREE

Genesis 2:9 - "In the middle of the garden were the tree of life and the tree of the knowledge of good and evil."

Genesis 3:2 - "God did say, 'You must not eat fruit from the tree that is in the middle of the garden, and you must not touch it, or you will die."

In the midst of the garden were two trees more beautiful and bountiful than all the others. The branches of the two trees hung like dark shadows that followed the movement of the wind, its thick leaves covering the branches as if some secret wanted to conceal itself.

The garden itself was a reservoir of special sounds out of which sublime silence trickled along with slow streams of small brooks, interrupted only by the soft cooing of doves and serene songs chirped by sparrows. Of course this appealed to Azazel's assiduous[1] appetite. As ♎ reached ♎ hairy hand to fetch some fruit, the Voice of Elyon was heard in Earth's garden for the first time since it and all of its inhabitants were created.

"Azazel."

Azazel froze and his wiry hair cockled up on the back of his neck, just as his hand reached the fruit.

"I recognize this voice, but why here?" ♎ thought while trying to collect ♎ composure. "Should I dare answer?"

"Azazel, where are you?" The Voice sounded like a rockslide as it rumbled through the garden.

Azazel wondered why Elyon would ask, 'where are

1 Dogged and unending. Voracious

you?' when it was apparent that ♍ already knew the answer.

"Why are you here is the question? You gave this garden to me. I demand you to depart now. You are not welcome here and are nothing more than a extraterrestrial trespasser. I allowed you here to tend this garden and mend your rebellious reputation. What you don't realize is, I am here to save you from eternal extermination."

"I think you are here to keep your secrets secure. Why are you so protective of your powers? You give me Earth and here you are to interfere with my interests."

Elyon was way beyond engaging in a word battle with a '*blustery bigot!*'

"I will say this twice, so my Word will be established on Earth. Do not touch the Tree of Life. Do not eat the fruit of the Tree containing the Knowledge of Good and Evil. Do not touch the Tree of Knowledge and do not eat of the Tree of Life. If you do, you will become an *'eternal being.'* Your wish of being like unto Me will be partially granted, but you will curse what you have learned when you desire to perish and cannot. However, you will remain forever alive as a spirit to suffer for your deeds."

Azazel stuck out ♎ forked tongue, "Now you are acting reasonably, rewarding me for guarding this garden. *'I will'*[1] not only touch, *'I will'* touch and eat the fruit of the Tree of Life and the Tree of Knowledge of Good and Evil. You have just given me two gifts I have greatly desired. Ahhh, life and knowledge are mine."

1 Isaiah 14:13-14 - "I will ascend to the heavens; I will raise my throne above the stars of God; I will sit enthroned on the mount of assembly, on the utmost heights of Mount Zaphon. I will ascend above the tops of the clouds; I will make myself like the Most High."
"I Will." Satan's two favorite words. Satan said, "I Will" 5 times in these three verses alone.

The Prodigal Satan

"Azazel, you must decide now; *will you become a devil or remain an angel, a destroyer or defender, be hellish or heroic, act as menace or messenger, become the viper or the victor*. The fate of many, the future of myriads will be determined by your decision."

"Just the way I like it," Azazel arrogantly answered.

Elyon's tone saddened, "My last Word to you is this, until now, you have not been held accountable for your actions, but once you taste of the knowledge of good and evil, you will understand who you are and what you are doing. You will become your own god (g).[1]

Everything you say or do from now on is 'willful' and you will be liable for every lie, every evil deed, deception or demagoguery you engage in. There will be no returning to your innocence that you are surrendering. *'Your greatest torment will be your revelation of what goodness is.'* Whether you confess truth or not, you will hauntingly know that I am *'good.'* This will plague you more than the knowledge of your own evil. You are guilty of committing reprehensible crimes against Me and all of creation, yet you deceive yourself that you are good and still remain defiant!"

Azazel shouted, "Amen," as ♑ wrapped ♑ thin fingers around a overhanging branch of the Tree of Life, violently shaking it, hoping to dislodge its fruit. As a piece of fruit fell, ♑ snatched it from the air spearing it with one swipe of ♑ elongated, self-sharpened fingernails and began gluttonously gorging ♑self, unknowingly devouring damnation and death. The unexpected happened, "Aaggggaaagg!" And again, "aaggggaaagg!" Satan puked. "You have poisoned me! Aaggggaaagg, huuukkk. I should have known you came here

1 ♑ - Symbol designating Azazel as god, chosen as symbol because of its resemblance to "No." Satan's "no" to God's commandments changed the plan of God forever. Used in place of personal pronouns such as he, she, his hers, etc.

to, huuukkk, to kill me, not to give me life. Aaggggaaagg!"

"You have poisoned yourself, Azazel and *'you cannot regurgitate rebellion out of your system.'* What you ingested has infectiously injured everything in the Heavens and on Earth. You will see, but you will not care.

Azazel was sickened and stunned!

This time it was the all powerful hand of Elyon that grabbed the trunks of the trees of knowledge and the tree of life, uprooting them with force, leaving huge holes in the earthly garden.

"You will never eat of the fruit of these trees again." With that said, Bene Elyon left Azazel looking up into the heavens wondering if ♈ would ever return to Earth.

CHAPTER FOURTEEN
THE ALTAR OF THE ALMIGHTY
SATAN'S OBLISK OF OBSESSION

Isaiah 19:19 - "In this period, there shall be an altar[1] of the YHWH in the middle of the land of Egypt, with the image of an idol in conjunction with or bordering the territory of darkness, all unto YHWH." Author's own translation!

Would this be the beginning of the Egyptians Zep Tepi, regarded as the mysterious golden age that immediately followed Creation? The Egyptian calendar begins with what is actually *'re-creation'* and they knew little of Emit, although they do worship "Sheshep-ankh known as the *'living image of Atum,'* their creator of the universe. Azazel craved to confiscate the identity of *"The express Image of the Invisible God."* Azazel's rule as god of this world[2] was *'a beginning'* all of its own.

♑ ordered ♑ Captains to conscript every angel under their command to come at once. They would begin to work on nothing else but solving the riddle of the symmetrical structure.

1 Isaiah spoke of the Pyramid: "In that day there shall be an altar to the Lord in the midst of the Land of Egypt, and a monument at the border thereof to the Lord, and it shall be for a sign, and for a witness unto the Lord of Hosts in the Land of Egypt". In the Hebrew language, each of the original 30 words has a numerical value because each Hebrew letter is also a number. When the 30 words are added up, the total is 5,449 that is the most significant number of the Pyramid. It is the exact height of the Pyramid in sacred Jewish inches.

2 2nd Corinthians 4:4 - "Satan, who is the god of this world, has blinded the minds of those who don't believe. They are unable to see the glorious light of the Good News. They don't understand this message about the glory of Christ, who is the exact likeness of God."

The Prodigal Satan

'Earth's possessor was possessed with the ❖.'[1]

Azazel ordered from a distance, "Abaddon you take your troops and approach the ❖ with care. It could be a trap set by Elyon to ensnare us."

Abaddon gave the signal and Satan's soldiers slowly advanced toward the ❖ not knowing what to expect. They moved ever so quietly, trusting if they made no noise the ❖ would not harm them. Even Azazel whispered so as not to be heard but by those standing closest to ♑.

"Nothing like this exists anywhere else. This has to be it; the rebus, the riddle, the rune,[2] in my possession."

"Its glimmer is even more glorious than it was from the heavens. It almost hurts. Do you feel it," Pythus susurrated.[3]

"There is a feeling here in this place, but I am not sure that it is the brightness of the structure that I feel."

The soldiers felt it too and it frightened them into falling back until Azazel screamed at them to stop. They were more afraid of Fuehrer[4] Azazel than their fear of a feeling. All that ♑ could do to persuade them to advance was to proceed toward the ❖ by ♑self.

Azazel rashly realized that ♑ was relinquishing the right to rule, by allowing Abaddon to be first to touch or enter the ❖.

"Abaddon, stop, stop and wait right where you are," Azazel commanded.

Abaddon was quick to obey the order, seeing ♎ was reluctant to advance and anxious to retreat.

1 Pyramid -The word pyramid is composed of the Greek word "pyra" meaning fire, light, or visible and the Greek word "midos" meaning measures. (Fiery measure)

2 A Mystery or a puzzle of numbers, words or characters.

3 Speak in a low tone.

4 Strongman or dictator

The Prodigal Satan

Azazel rushed past Abaddon like a rabid dog on the attack, as all anxiously awaited to see what would happen.

Carefully, ♑ reached out ♑ trembling hand to touch the towering triangle, similarly shaking as ♑ did while tasting the fruit of the Tree of Life. Only this time, Azazel trembled in fear not with excitement.

"Ieeeee," ♑ bellowed out violently jerking his hand away.

Abaddon, ran toward Azazel, but stopped short upon seeing the strangest sight. "Azazel, what is happening to you?"

"What do you mean by what is happening to me?"

Belial arrived just in time to intervene, "Just wait now, Abaddon...!" "Azazel, it is apparent something we don't understand just happened to you."

Before anything else could be said, Azazel purposefully brushed ♑ hand against the smooth surface of the highly polished stone of the ❖. Instantly, ♑ entire body illuminated to the point that Belial and Abaddon startled, backing away from ♑. Azazel wanted to see for ♑self what the others had observed.

"This is the work of ♈. He already knows how I hate the light and this is His way of stopping ♑ from learning His secrets."

Pythus stood close by and could hear the discouragement in Azazel's tone of voice. Using his usual gift of gab, ♎ encouraged, "♑ don't be deterred. We will not be defeated by this distraction. It came to me as you devoured the fruit of the tree of knowledge of good and evil, that we can use both evil and good to accomplish our aims. If it is anticipated that we are always evil, then none will ever expect us to do good. If we can use good to advance our cause then why not?"

Azazel's body dimmed as ♑ listened intently. "Yes, yes, yes," ♑ shouted louder each time ♑ darkened." ♈ is caught in His own snare once again."

"You are the Angel of darkness and the Angel of light. The most magnificent of all creatures," Pythus added.

For the first time, Azazel realized ♑ possessed a dual nature; and *'how well suited ♑ was for deception.'*

Azazel is the darkest of demons by nature, but transforms into an angel of light when it's convenient.

♑ screamed, "Light, you are my enemy, but also my greatest tool." *'I don't like you, but I love you. I don't want you, but I need you!'*

Beelzebub lifted up, levitating ♎self above the apex of the ❖, closely surveying the structure, but intentionally avoiding contact with the ❖. Eventually, every demon would have an encounter with the ❖. For Beelzebub, it was now!

"This is not one stone. They are fit together as...as...as? As what?" ♎ questioned ♎self.

♎ had no point of reference. *'Everything else was primitive compared to this pyramid.'* As ♎ reached the pinnacle, the wonderment of the workmanship distracted Beelzebub just enough that ♎ pinions brushed the gilded gold capstone. An electrifying shock sent ♎ soaring so high that ♎ feared ♎ had been caught in the vortex of a wormhole transporting ♎ back to Rahab or beyond.

The horde watching from the ground wondered and worried for the well-being of Beelzebub, but more so were taken by the mystery and thrill of the towering triptych[1]. Little did any demon know that they were standing at *'the Altar of the Almighty!'*

1 Triangle or set of three.

CHAPTER FIFTEEN
THE PYTHAGOREAN THEOREM[1]

Psalms 147:4 - "He counts the number of the stars; He gives names to all of them."

Beelzebub was breathless after ♎ brush with banishment from below, but with a huff, ♎ managed to blurt out a word of revelation, "Ganita."[2] "The squares," ♑ uttered. "It's the squares. Each of them would be the same shape as the giant structure if I could cut them in half from one corner to another."

Leviathan scoffed, "You must be reeling from your unwanted flight Beelzebub. We have no idea what you are saying."

Mammon spoke up, "I do and I believe in what ♎ saw and in what ♎ is saying. When Azazel spoke to me of understanding wealth, I came to the conclusion that there must be some method of making it valuable. I remembered hearing ♍ use language I was not familiar with. ♍ *'called it counting.'* ♍ counted everything that ♍ made, just as you, Azazel require of me to do with our..." ♎ caught ♎self. "Sorry, I meant your wealth. Stop and think, Bene Elyon gave us each our names, which means we are separate but yet together, just like the squares. He must have counted us too."

Not known for ♎ mental mastery, Leviathan leaped in, "I told you. See, look at the slabs." ♎ pointed from a safe distance, still timid about touching the ❖. "They are evenly

1 A mathematical equation related to the three triangles of a pyramid. The theorem has numerous proofs possibly the most of any mathematical theorem, some dating back thousands of years.

2 Oldest known word meaning 'mathematics.' Derived for the oldest known written language, Sanskrit.

and tightly joined and held there by some strange substance. If we are going to get at what this thing means, it is going to take ganita. We must learn to count and reckon."

Azazel stood quietly with ♑ hand under ♑ sharp chin stroking ♑ stringy hair, not knowing where this would go.

Mammon continued with a hint of ill in ♎ voice, while making a clearing noise in ♎ throat to emphasize ♎ irritation for the interruption; "Call it ganita if we will, but *'more important than naming is numbering.'* We must come up with our own system of sums."

Azazel availed ♑self of ♑ thieving ability to steal the suggestion that a system of numbering was the key to the knowledge of Elyon. ♑ pride compelled ♑ to claim to be the originator a system of counting, even though ♑ despised the true creator of the concept.

The cord tied around ♑ waist was still red!

The Prodigal Satan

CHAPTER SIXTEEN
THE SEER TURNED SINGER
PIPPING THE TUNE OF THE PUZZLE

 [1]

Though Azazel would take full credit for mathematics, ♑ understood that ♑ did not have the intellect to invent ganita, so ♑ summoned Dudael.[2] Dudael was the only Ophanim to rebel against Elyon, and Azazel remained wary of ♎. Azazel's uneasiness was due to Dudael possessing so many eyes and having been employed so close to Elyon's throne. It was strongly suspicioned that the Ophanim has special powers related to their vision.

"Dudael, I have need of you, but I must be sure of your loyalty, being as you as an Ophanim are alone here on earth with me. You are a *'throne toter,'* yet you forsook your highly regarded position to rebel against Elyon."

"I was wondering if you would ever notice me? I have envied Abaddon, Leviathan, Beelzebub and others that you rely on. What may I do to be of service to you, my new lord?"

"It's your eyes. The light that comes from them is different from that of any of us. Its beams are straight and piercing. I have watched carefully and you are able to look in many directions at one time. I have even observed your beams crossing and forming the shape of the structure that we are here to study."

1 In Music, this is what "divisive rhythm" looks like when drawn as a pattern. Do you see the music of Pyramids?

2 Dudael - Name meaning, "The one who pierces (by seeing), or breaks through."

"Yes, this is true, but does this help anything."

"I don't know yet. I just want you to look at the ❖ and then look and look again. Look at the shapes. Open your mind and let's see what happens. What ever you see, I want you to make symbols representing the images. Bring the symbols to me and me only."

Azazel intently watched, as Dudael sat gazing at the pyramid, light shooting from ♎ manifold eyes in every direction, bouncing off of the shiny surface of the triangular surface and reflecting deep into the darkness of the heavens. Dudael selected a flat piece of sandstone and a sharp piece of granite and began chipping away, evidently recording ♎ findings. The ricocheting radiance of light and the sound of stone on stone brought every rebel demon to the site, peering to see the spectacle of the search for the mystery of the ❖.

Without warning Dudael fell backwards, dropping ♎ stone chisel, as ♎ breathlessly uttered, "Ganita!"

Azazel and Abaddon rushed to see what happened to Dudael, only to find ♎ somewhat incoherent, singing in some strange language, fervently repeating the same words as foam bubbled out of the sides of ♎ mouth, even as ♎ lips revealed a grin of sublime satisfaction.

Dudael sang,"Ukta, atyukta, madhya, pratistha, supratistha, gayatri, usnik, pankti, tristubh, zota."[1]

What happened next, shocked the sensibility of every demon standing close enough to hear. Azazel's pipes fell silent for the first time since the descent to Earth. Without a queue, ♑ musical body began playing in perfect pitch with the song of Dudael. "Ukta, atyukta, madhya, pratistha, supratistha, gayatri, usnik, pankti, tristubh, zota."

Pythus was the first to begin swaying to the sound of Azazel's hypnotic music, but soon joined by the rest of the

1 Close to the sanscrit words for one through ten. Author's slight alteration.

restless rabble in what became *gyrating, self-gratifying gamboling.*[1] Their reaction was not lost on Azazel. ♑ discovered a powerful tool that ♑ continues to use to move the masses and persuade multitudes of ♑ politics.

The din of the *'Demonic Duet'* filled the gardens of Elysian Fields. Their song disclosed the secrets of God, the music divulged the mysteries of God, their score broadcast that the clue to the ❖, was concealed in chords of music and *'Azazel had tuned in.'*

The cord tied around ♑ waist was still red!

1 Cut loose, kick up one's heels.

The Prodigal Satan

CHAPTER SEVENTEEN
UNHOLY HIEROGLYPHICS[1]

Galileo Galilei (1564-1642) said, "The universe cannot be read until we have learned the language and become familiar with the characters in which it is written. It is written in mathematical language, and the letters are triangles, circles and other geometrical figures, without which means it is humanly impossible to comprehend a single word.

Pythus picked up the slab of sandstone that Dudael dropped and to ♎ astonishment it contained something completely unknown to ♎, one of most perceptive and discerning demons.

"Azazel, stop your music and look at this."

Azazel was leery of taking ♎ eyes off of Dudael, but Pythus insisted. "Lord!" No response. "Lord Azazel, look." "You need to look at this right now."

"Don't bother me now. Without Dudael, I may never learn the secret of El..." Stopping in mid sentence, a look of disgust came over Azazel. ♑ teetered on the edge of allowing ♑ own words to betray ♑ insecurity concerning ♑ godhood. "Maybe I should leave the speech making to Pythus," ♑ muttered. ♑ felt the eyes of every demon staring at ♑, as though they heard what ♑ almost accidentally said.

Azazel knew that one misspoken word could destroy ♑ kingdom. ♑ cursed under ♑ breath, "*<*#%*@#%* demons. They seem to be waiting to find a reason to revolt against me as they have Elyon. I wonder which of them wishes to replace me?"

At the insistence of Pythus, Azazel turned from Dudael to see what so intrigued ♎. The music stopped and Dudael

1 Hieroglyphics - Means "Holy Carvings."

roused from ♎ stupor.

"What are these strange markings?" Pythus inquired.

"Azazel was stupefied and had to be rescued by a groggy Dudael. *"These are holy carvings. Look closely, your ganita in shapes. Let me show you what I have eyed and etched for you my lord."*

Out of pride, Azazel proposed, "You do mean, what I have sung and not only what you have seen, don't you?"

"Yes, my lord and you sang it so superbly. Now, may I continue?"

"With my permission. Of course. Proceed."

Dudael placed his finger over the first of the hieroglyphically carved figures carefully tracing its outline. "First, I saw this shape, like unto the planetary stones that shine throughout the heavens. The Earth stone on which we stand has no sharp points or edges as does this ❖ that rises up before us."

"Does not sound like much of a revelation to me," Azazel quipped still edgy over the last few moments of conversation.

"Undaunted, Dudael pressed on, "What I saw looked like this. O I was told to call it Zotah."[1] The stones of the ❖ surely have come from the earth in the shape of zotah but have been altered to become angles."[2] I call the sharp points angles, because Elyon claims ♍ created us as angels. This was ♍ devious way of putting ♍ signature on us. ♍ ended our name like the beginning of ♍ name, 'EL.' Angles are our doing, so I propose we take ♍ 'el' signature off of us, not to be ♍ angels, but called angles which will unlock the secrets of Elyon."

Dudael confidently added, "We know not how the stones were altered, but soon, my eyes will reveal the secret."

1 Sanskrit language meaning 1-10. Author's word zota added for 0.

2 Angle - Shape formed by two lines meeting at a point.

The Prodigal Satan

"Ukta was the second shape that I saw. It has but 1 angle. Then I saw other shapes and I heard their names in this order." Atyukta has 2 angles, Madhya has 3, Pratistha has 4 angles, Supratistha 5, Gayatri 6, Usnik 7, Pankti 8 and Tristubh 9 has angles. This is what my eyes saw and measured. All the shapes of the pyramid are in the ganita."

"Brilliant Dudael, absolutely brilliant. You did hear me sing didn't you?"

"Yes lord, I did hear you sing, but it get's even better."

"How so, Dudael," Azazel demanded as ♑ tired of Dudael being the center of attention.

"This is where you become god Azazel," Dudael announced with arrogance as ♎ spread ♎ eagle like wings, roared with lion-like growl and stomped the earth like a wild ox. "Ganita is endlessly eternal. Just keep adding zotahs, uktas, atyuktas or tristubhs and you will have the universe. It doesn't end. Use these combinations and the heavens will open to you. Nothing can be hidden or concealed."

Azazel's demeanor calmed as thoughts of Godhood possessed ♑ poisonous mind. Besides, Dudael had been a *'throne toter'* in Elyon's kingdom and should know a god when ♎ *'sees'* one. "I will keep ♎ close and ♎ can carry my throne. Dudael will be a valuable slave!"

Azazel's massive body pulsed with rhythmic music as *"the hostile host of heaven"* sang their new song, the *"altered anthem of arithmetic."* "Ukta, atyukta, madhya, pratistha, supratistha, gayatri, usnik, pankti, tristubh, zota. Ukta, atyukta, madhya, pratistha, supratistha, gayatri, usnik, pankti, tristubh, zota." Out with *'the Old hymn of heaven.'* With sin came a strange stanza. *'The Celestial chorus Holy, Holy, Holy was banned from the band. No more music for the Master!'*

The crimson cord around Azazel's waist was still red!

CHAPTER EIGHTEEN
ENTRANCE TO ELYON'S ALTAR

"We are well on our way to understanding the exterior, but I am sure that you must have seen from the ground, what I saw from the air."

"Beelzebub, don't speak in riddles with me," Azazel snapped. "You are talking about the opening on the side of the ❖ aren't you?"

"Yes my lord, there is an opening but I have no idea where it leads or what will happen if anyone enters."

"Stop Beelzebub, stop right there. Surely you aren't suggesting that I am fearful of taking flight into the ❖."

"No Azazel." Beelzebub thought, "enough of this lord stuff," but managed to hold back. ♎ rebutted with a tempered tone of temper. "I am not suggesting that you are fearful, but I do confess that I fear for you. Remember what happened when you first touched the ❖." This was a critical moment and Azazel had learned, *'no crisis should be wasted.'* Crisis and fear were to be ♑ mainstay.

"Fear itself is great power," ♑ preached. "It moves me to do marvelous things and I will use it to get what I want. Remember what I am telling you. I will be feared more than this ❖!"

"Beelzebub sensed it was sensible to back off for now."

"Abaddon, bring Dudael. We are going in."

Belial stepped in with ♎ usual fawning flattery. "No one should doubt you Azazel. You will succeed as always in flawless fashion."

Mammon hastily arrived to add, "With permission I will accompany you. Surely the fortune of '*Elyon's Favorite Planet*' is hidden somewhere in this heap of stones."

"And go you must Mammon. Have you mastered ganita yet?"

"I have and can repeat the names of every number. Let me show you, "Ukta, atyukta, madhya, pratistha..."

"Alright!" Azazel disdainfully shouted. "Enough of the cheap chatter. On to the next lesson. I have figured out how to use math to measure the ❖ using my body. It came to me to use the dimensions of my body to understand how the ❖is constructed. Mammon, as we walk together inside the ❖, I want you to watch my feet. I will walk and not levitate at all, stepping as I place one foot against the other. You count and record my footsteps. This is the method that we will use to map the ❖. I will tell you more later about my ukta atyukta (12) toes, but I don't want to overload you. Let's go discover Elyon's secrets!" They required no light, because each of them sparkled the moment they touched the ❖.

Dudael led the way, with Azazel close behind and Mammon right on ♑ heels. Azazel's light was noticeably brighter than those who accompanied ♑, it casting a macabre shadow all around the narrow entrance of the ❖.

After traversing a short distance, the eager explorers came upon an intersection. Several of Dudael's eyes shot laser like beams up the shaft veering slightly to the right. Some of ♎ eyes focused on the passage that was generally straight ahead, but most of ♎ optics opted to look back, dreading what might lurk behind them more so that which lay ahead.

With precision, Dudael quickly reported, "The shaft to the right ascends. The shaft ahead of us leads downward."

"Straight ahead." Azazel's nervous voice was low pitched, but it reverberated off the rock walls betraying ♑ anxiety. It was not *'straight'* that appealed to ♑, proven by the fact that ♑ became known as the *'crooked serpent.'* [1] ♑ unintentionally displayed ♑ *"disposition for down."*

Azazel's chest pounded wildly, "We are close. Elyon's treasures are down here. ♍ stacked these stones to bury ♍ secrets, thinking that I would never find them."

"Supratistha zota, (50) supratistha ukta, (51) supratistha atyukta, (52) supratistha madhya (53)." Mammon methodically counted while hoping not to lose track as Azazel carefully placed one foul foot in front of another.

Dudael's stopped suddenly. His eyes did not deceive ♎. A dark wall detected some distance away meant a dead end. "Azazel, I believe that we have come to the end of this shaft."

They would soon find out that it was not the end, but rather an entrance into a cramped chamber, its main feature being an open shaft in its center. The chasm became known as *'the bottomless pit.'* Those who had the misfortune to fall, or worse be cast into it, were never seen again.

"Press on, Dudael. Something must be down here."

"Blind obedience" became easy as with a few more steps, every demon went pitch black. They were engulfed in an eerie ebonic gloom, usually comfortable for them, but this was different. The sudden onset of the onyx blackness was not just the absence of light. It suggested that the demons were outside of the ❖, but if so, where?

In the ensuing confusion, someone or something let out a chilling cry. From whom, no one knew or cared, but the ensuing clamor turned chaotic as they thrashed about in terror. In panic, they pushed and grabbed one another, resulting in some stumbling and falling headlong into the confined chamber. The unfortunate were swallowed down the narrow shaft, disappearing as the echoes of their wailings

1 Job 26:13- "By his breath the skies were fair; his hand pierced the crooked serpent."

faded into a fatal stillness.

Belial bumbled backwards into the ❖'s portal, breaking the grip of gloominess as ♎ body lit up. "Over here," ♎ beckoned. ♎ did not need to beg. *'The spooked spelunkers'*[1] scurried to get away from the mysterious snaring shaft!

The first foray into the ❖ was a failure as the group quickly retraced their steps counting them from the point of light back to the exit.

With bated breath, Mammon reported, "Gayatri gayatri (66) of your feet Azazel, exactly sixty-six. Mammon looked around, "Azazel...Azazel?"

Azazel had not waited around for a math lesson.

The crimson cord was still red!

1 One who explores caves or dark confined spaces.

The Prodigal Satan

CHAPTER NINETEEN
PYTHUS THE PREACHER
THE SACRED SERMON

Matthew 4:6 - "If you are the Bene Elyon, he said, throw yourself down. For it is written: He will command his angels concerning you, and they will lift you up in their hands, so that you will not strike your foot against a stone."

"Are you ever going back in," Pythus questioned? "If not, I must be thinking of what to tell the others so that they will not think you to be weak."

Pythus was quickly learning the meaning of Azazel's guttural growl and anticipated the verbal abuse that surely was coming. Instead, Azazel cleared ♑ throat so hard that ♑ almost choked when ♑ started to speak.

"Yes, uhumm, humm, yes I am. I did not risk everything to leave this Earth without something to show for it."

"Azazel, it's time to take a risk. I suggest that you must succeed soon or at least show some progress, as the demons are demanding it."

" Demanding! Demanding what? What have you heard?"

"They say openly, your desires are selfish, your motives suspicious, your demands excessive and your directions errant."

"Do you agree with them in their assessment of me?"

"Agree with the imbeciles? Never! In fact, I believe if anything, you are being to soft on them. They will soon believe you are easy like Elyon, but for all the wrong reasons."

"Not that I, the Subtle Satan, need anyone to advise me, but if we are just talking, what would you suggest I do?"

"Just suggesting, I would use these fiends to finish

what you came here to do. Forget their complaints and coerce them to do your bidding by favor or by force." Indeed, you must go back into the ❖ and its secrets will succumb to your stubbornness. Just one more suggestion?"

"I suppose."

"As you learn the secrets of Elyon, you should build your own monuments. Right here." Pythus stomped ♎ foot several times for emphasis. "Right here, on this spot next to the ❖. Build something bigger, build it better, build as many as you like. Come with me," Pythus politely invited.

They levitated up to the gold and silver laden pinnacle of the ❖, which seemed to pulse with energy upon their arrival. As they gazed out over the garden of Elysian Fields, it was brimming with multitudes of misguided Malakim meaninglessly meandering around.

It was quite a moment for Pythus, "lord Azazel, behold your Kingdom and your slaves. You aspire to attain godhood and for others to worship you. *'Worship yourself first.'* Behave like the Maker, the owner of all. The fullness of the Earth is yours." "These demons," Pythus pointed as he pirouetted in every direction, "you have the power to possess them. Own them and they will obey you. Even if you should cast yourself down from here, they would bear you up at risk of their own well-being. They will serve you as slaves and cut stones for you to build your own ❖. Why? Because you will control their food. Turn their cut stones into bread for them in this manner. No stones, no food. If they don't work, they will not eat."

Standing atop the lofty height of the ❖, Azazel experienced an unearthly epiphany, envisioning exactly how ♑ would rule the planet, which was and is the Crown Jewel of Elyon's Emit.

Azazel declared, "I will."

The Prodigal Satan

CHAPTER TWENTY
THE PYRAMIDICAL PLANETARIUM
ANCIENT ASTRONOMERS

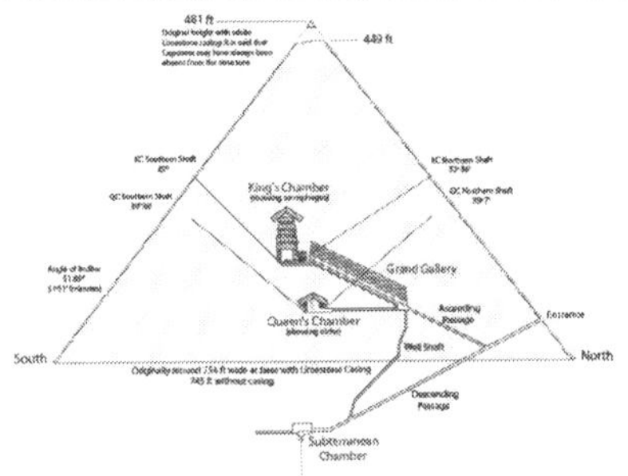

The Internal Features of the Great Pyramid of Giza shown in Cross Section looking West (Drawn to Scale)
Diagram by Gary Osborn. © Copyright 2003. All Rights Reserved.

"We mortals being prisoners of time, peep through our telescopes, hoping to peer into our far away future, oblivious of the fact we are staring at our starry past." Louis Green

Dudael was quick to report, "I have completed much of the work of ganita.

Azazel was quicker to note, "Nothing would be known or completed with me adding the finishing touches to the trigonometric calculations. I used my foot, and my thumbs on my six fingered hands to discover the *'Inch.'*[1]"

Using math, we can now measure our way into the mystical modus operandi[2] of Elyon."

With this powerful knowledge came the confidence to

1 In some other languages, the word for "inch," is similar to or the same as the word for "thumb"; for example, French: pouce inch/thumb; Italian: pollice inch/thumb; Spanish: pulgada inch, pulgar thumb; Swedish: tum inch, tumme thumb; Given the etymology of the word "inch," it would seem that the inch is a unit derived from the foot unit in Latin in Roman times.

2 A Latin phrase, translated as "method of operation."

return to the interior of Ikhet.

Taking the advice of Pythus, Azazel sent surveyors into every tunnel, corridor, room and opening of the ❖. To take ownership of the ❖, Belial suggested, "We should change the name of the ❖ to *'Ikhet,'* meaning the *'Glorious Light.'* See how the ❖ brightens and at times goes dark? Likewise Ikhet has a dual meaning, the first refers to the ❖ and the second, to Azazel, who can appear at will as an angel of *'Inglorious illumination.'*

Instead of being flattered, Azazel literally flew into a rage, lifting up and crashing down to Earth at the use of the word *'second'* in referring to ♑.

With quick wit Pythus stated, "Your lordship, I meant to say *'next'* not second. We know that you are second to none!"

The many mysterious mathematical configurations challenged Azazel's council who were appointed to cipher the collected calculations.

Dudael being head of the committee commenced, "I'll start. We know the number of the stones covering the exterior of Ikhet, but still do not know their meaning."

"What is the number," Azazel inquired?

"Ukta pratistha pratistha, zota zota zota. (144,000)

Azazel may not be fluent of speech, but ♑ has an astounding aptitude for arithmetic.

Without hesitation ♑ boasted, "How easy. I have used my feet and hands to unlock the secret of ganita." Under ♑ breath ♑ muttered, *'demon dunces.'*

"Look, ♑ demonstrated, holding up one hand and kicking one leg up showing off one of ♑ hulking feet. What do you see," ♑ crackled.

Abaddon sheepishly said, "Gayatri (6) fingers and gayatri (6) toes."

"And how many does that make, Abaddon?"

The Prodigal Satan

"I am a soldier and not a student," Abaddon replied as ♎ yellow eyes glowered with the heat of being ridiculed.

"Well Commander, perhaps you should study strategy. Our enemy Elyon evidently knows ganita and our final battle with ♍ will likely involve numbers. Let me show you. Atyukta (2) hands, ukta atyukta (12) fingers. Atyukta (2) feet, ukta atyukta (12) toes. 12 x 12 = 144. It is a number of completion, just as I am complete from my hands to my feet. The Ikhet represents something complete and perfect, but on an unknown scale, thus the madhya (3) added zota's (000). We started with ganita gayatri (6) and ended with ganita zota, zota, zota. I am sure that Elyon has ♍ own number, so I choose gayatri, gayatri, gayatri (666)[1] to display my power and perfection!

The council sat silent in subdued awe.

The silence was broken when Azazel began to applaud ♑self, continuing until the council felt constrained to join in. When the council members expected that their hands would fall off from clapping, Azazel mercifully solicited, "Any questions?"

None dared to speak until Dudael courageously continued ♎ report. "As you know lord Azazel, the entrance to Ikhet faces toward one of the great '*sketchings in the sky.*' The symbol resembling the Lion face of the Chayot. Could this mean that a Lion god controls the entrance to Ikhet?"

"No god beside me will control the Ikhet and not just the Ikhet, but all the Earth. I will be '*the Lion that walks to and fro upon the face of the earth*'[2] and '*sits upon the north side*[3] *entrance of Ikhet!*'" "That settles that. Continue."

1 Revelation 13:18 - "This calls for wisdom. Let the person who has insight calculate the number of the beast, for it is the number of a man. That number is 666."

2 1st Peter 5:8 - Satan walks to and fro on the earth.

3 Isaiah 14:13 - Satan sits on the North side of the Mount of God.

"Concerned about the pit with no bottom, we searched the corridor leading upward. This passageway is inclined and extremely narrow, only pratistha (4) feet high, but quite long, extending tristubh pankti (98) feet until it opens into a grand gallery. The grand gallery is atyukta pankti (28) feet high,

Madhya point pratistha (3.4) feet wide and ukta supratistha usnik (157) feet in length. It is very strange why this passageway opens so widely for no apparent reason."

"Not to worry Dudael, I will know when the time comes."

"The mystery is much more complex than just the corridors. Before we entered the grand gallery, there was a narrow passage angling off to one side toward the center of Ikhet. It led to a small chamber. We were very apprehensive about entering, thinking it might contain another opening to the bottomless pit."

With a chilled tone of unconcern Azazel callously remarked, "Evidently it did not. I see you standing before me."

Retorting with ♎ own tone of cynicism, Dudael carried on, "You will be glad that I am alive when I finish telling you what we found in there. First, the stones that formed the ceiling were cut at a small angle, but what we found next is the most interesting."

Azazel rubbed ♑ hands together and licked his dark lips in anticipation.

"There were two shafts cut on different angles, pointing upward out of the small chamber. Each one of them was marked with a symbol. The one facing the same direction as the opening into the Ikhet was marked like this, ♌."[1]

Dudael had etched ♌ on some soft stone.

"What this means, we have no idea," Dudael added.

Azazel looked disgusted and ♑ words proved it. "You

1 ♌ Symbol representing the Great Lion.

imbeciles. What would become of you without me? You tell me that the Ikhet's entrance and the shaft point in the same direction and yet you cannot reveal what the symbol means. As you stand at the entrance to the grand gallery and the small chamber, looking upward out of the entrance, what do you see in the heavens?"

"As we reported, we see the bright stars aligned artistically in the heavens, appearing as *'The great Lion.'*"

"Of course you do! I am the great Lion, written of on the *'black canvas of the heavens.'* As it is in heaven so shall it be here on the Earth. I am the entrance and the way to knowledge. The first ♌ symbol speaks of me and this is the key to understanding the other symbols."

"What else did you see," Azazel asked rhetorically.

"We could not see out of either shaft leading from the small chamber, but we do know that the second shaft pointed..."

"Toward the great heavenly Bull," Azazel butted in.

"It absolutely does, but how did you know?"

"Here, give me the soft stone and let me show you what you saw in the small chamber."

Dudael, Pythus and a few others pushed as close as they could to peer over Azazel's towering shoulder to see as ♑ quickly etched out a symbol identical to the one in the small chamber.

Needlessly, ♑ invited the onlookers to look." ♉[1]

"That is it! Exactly," they exclaimed!

Now they were fearful of asking how ♑ knew. They were beginning to believe that Azazel truly was God. *'Who has the right to question a God?'*

Azazel broke the tense lingering silence, "Were there other shafts pointed toward the heavens?"

1 ♉ symbol representing the great bull.

The Prodigal Satan

"Yes, there are two more that we found as we entered another larger chamber. These shafts were completely open to the outside of the Ikhet with a perfect view of certain of the brightest stones in the heavens."

"Ready yourselves. Take me to this chamber now. If I am right and who would doubt that I am, I know what I will see." Azazel snatched the soft stone from Dudael's grasp and began furiously scratching away with the hard pointed rock.

♑ held up the etched stone. "See? Each of you, watch and bear witness to my knowledge and that there is none like Azazel on Earth or in the heavens."

This is what ♑ chiseled out. ♏[1] and ♐.[2]

"What do these symbols mean?" Dudael pried.

"It is inconceivable to me that you, Dudael, and those who see you cannot perceive what these shafts are telling us. Do you not recognize your own body? Your appearance is like unto the lion, the ox, the eagle and the malakim. *Your shape, your form speak to who I am. I am on display in your design, painted in the positioning of the planets, sketched by the shining of the stars and shown in the secrets of this ❖. There is none like me. I am the Ukta and the Zota, the first and the last."*

Hurriedly, they made their way until they stood in the massive upper chamber deep in the interior of Ikhet.

Upon entering, Azazel noticed large bumps raising up on ♑ skin causing ♑ to tingle all over. "There is a feeling, a force in this room," ♑ said with a shiver as ♑ attempted to rub the bumps away.

There was a strange object in the center of the chamber, but Azazel hardly noticed, being distracted by ♑ determination to display ♑ discernment to the dumbfounded demons. ♑

1 ♏ symbol representing the great Eagle.

2 ♐ symbol representing Elyon's greatest creation, man.

positioned ♑self by the shaft to ♑ right. By holding ♑ soft stone etching next to the symbol on the wall of the ❖, the full effect of his knowledge would be on display.

"♏ on the wall. ♏ on my stone." "There, right before your eyes. The symbol that surely represents nothing else but an Eagle. Move out of my way. Move, move quickly."

Not knowing what Azazel wanted, but afraid to displease ♑ in any way caused the confused crew to stumble over one another getting out of ♑ way. Azazel was more than eager to look out of *'Elyon's telescope.'*

"Aha, there it is, the flaming stone *'Altair.'*[1] The monstrous Eagle of the heavens. The glory of *'Pleiades.'*[2] Look Pythus. See for yourself. Did any of you even think to look through the shaft?"

They were busy taking turns looking at Altair and mumbling, "We told Azazel that the shaft was open. How would we know that if we didn't look? At risk of danger, Belial shouted in a shrill voice, "I am tiring of being classed as inferior and unfairly called names such as imbecile."

Fortunate for Belial, Azazel had ♑ face pressed against the shaft on the opposite side of the large chamber and did not hear the rant.

Azazel spun around, "You imbeciles, stop your useless mumbling and get over here so that I can instruct you of matters important to a God. Look at my etching and this wall. ♐ - ♐ "Look up the shaft and you will see *'Rigel'*[3] the star of the Malakim and the glory of *'Orion.'*"[4]

1 ALTAIR (Alpha Aquilae). The 13th brightest star in the sky and the Alpha star of Aquila the Eagle.

2 Job 38:31 - "Can you bind the chains of the Pleiades? Can you loosen Orion's belt?

3 Rigel - The brightest star in Orion, 'the man, the hunter'.

4 Amos 5:8 - "He who made the Pleiades and Orion, who turns midnight into dawn and darkens day into night."

CHAPTER TWENTY-ONE
A GRAVE[1] FIT FOR A GOD

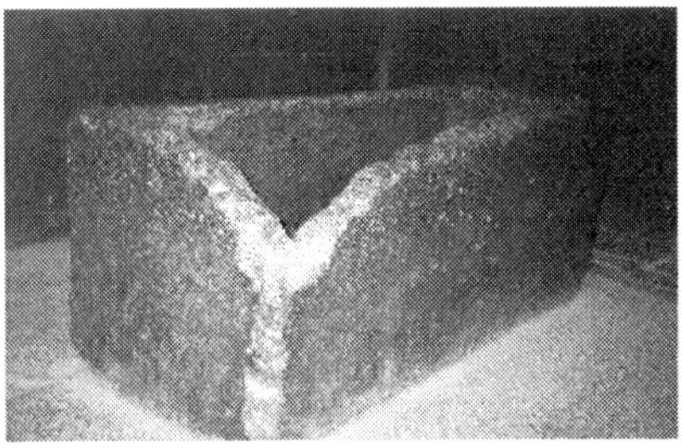

Azazel had a hard time calming down from ♑ exhilarating experience with the four shafts. ♑ would not confess it, but the fact that the two shafts of the small chamber were closed off was perturbing. A greater mystery was standing in center of the chamber with ♑ and yet ♑ overlooked it at first. This mysterious granite box, 'The Ark'[2] would test ♑ claim to be 'The All Knowing God!'

"Who put that here?" Azazel challenged.

The brazen general Abaddon was the only one with courage to say, "Azazel, the granite box was there when ♑ entered the chamber."

Dudael gained courage, "Lord, we have measured and there is no way that anyone brought the box in here. It is cut from one solid piece of stone and is larger than the passage way that leads into this chamber!"

"You measured?"

"Yes, we did. The ark measures pankti (8) feet long madhya (3) feet and part of a foot across and madhya (3) feet

1 Picture of Sarcophagus inside King's chamber of Great Pryamid.

2 The word Ark, "Aron" in Hebrew, means merely a chest but has been translated as 'coffin' in Genesis 50.26.

and a part of a foot in height."

"What about the capstone? Has it been moved?"

"No! Not one of us dared to move it, not knowing what might lurk beneath the capstone."

Azazel was certain that this was the moment when every secret of Elyon, Bene Elyon, Michael, Gabriel or any other power of the heavens would become ♑.

"Abaddon, you and the others; lift the capstone." "Now!" ♑ barked.

They slowly slid the capstone to one side, carefully resting it on top of the ark until all usnik (6) had a good grip and they gently placed it on the warm floor of the chamber.

Of course Azazel was the first to look inside. He spread his long arms the full length of the ark to hold everyone else back, in case there should be some treasure or secret to keep for ♑self.

♑ arms drooped and fell to ♑ side in disappointment. "Empty." "There is absolutely nothing in there."

The rest of the crew scurried to look.

"Do none of you trust me? I said, there is nothing in there."

"My lord, it had nothing to do with trust. We are curious as you are," Pythus consoled.

"Put the capstone back in place. It will come to me. I know it will. Just as the other mysteries were mastered by me. The answer will come. It will. It will!"

CHAPTER TWENTY- TWO
THE CRYPTOGRAM IN THE CRYPT

As Abaddon and ♎ helpers picked up the capstone, not realizing there was a top and bottom side, they placed the capstone on top the ark the opposite way they had found it. They inadvertently exposed evidence that would lead to an explanation of 'Elyon's cryptic crypt.'

Azazel started down the long corridor leading out of Ikhet, when ♑ heard the excited echo of Beelzebub's voice, "Azazel, come back up here. Come, we have something for you to see."

"What now?" ♑ hissed as ♑ traipsed up the tunnel.

"Look, Azazel. Some etchings, but not of your symbols."

"Im looking, I'm looking, can't you see, I'm looking," Azazel spewed angrily, *'ticked at feeling tricked.'*

There were the letters *'noylezaza.'* All that Azazel could think to do was to copy them and hope it was not too obvious that ♑ had no idea what this meant.

"Dudael, take my stone and etch out these letters. Bring the written stone to me and no one else is to have a copy. Abaddon turn the capstone over to the position in which you found it. I don't want the letters showing."

Dudael delivered the etched stone as ordered, but Azazel was not through with ♎.

"Dudael, I am going to lie down upon the earth and I want you to measure me with your feet."

"As you please Master."

"Ukta, atyukta, madhya, pratistha, supratistha, gayatri, usnik, and part of pankti. Just over usnik (6) feet in length Master. Why such a strange request."

"Measure my width and I will tell you."

"But I cannot measure your width without stepping on you."

"Dudael, take a stick and make a mark on each side of me. Then, I will get up and you walk between the marks.

Dudael flushed bright red at ♎ own stupidity. "I hope ♑ doesn't call me imbecile."

Azazel snickered!

"Ukta, atyukta, madhya. Just barely over madhya feet. Now, please tell me your reason."

"Do these measurements remind you of anything else you recently measured?"

"Huh, let me think. Hummm, I've got it, the Ark. The Ark is almost the same size."

"Just big enough for me to fit into and I believe that is what I am meant to do. I just need to find out why before I do. Leave me for now. I will summon you and the others when I am ready to go back in."

Azazel remembered the experience that g had with Beelzebub at the pinnacle of the ❖. This would be a likely place to go for g to explore the enigma of the Ark.

With no one around to hear, ♑ said aloud, "For once I desire the light to enlighten me."

Elyon heard Azazel's words from the lofty heights of ♍ distant throne. Sadly it was *'a helpless, hopeless hope'* felt in Heaven. According to the demands of Grace, The Logos decided to allow Satan to share some of the *'secrets of the Sacred altar.'*

Azazel took the etched stone and went to the pinnacle to ponder the meaning of the hidden message carved on the capstone of the Ark. The gold and silver covered stone sitting atop the ❖ seemed unusually brilliant.

"Let me see, n-o-y-l-e-z-a-z-a," ♑ slowly and repeatedly rehearsed. To ♑ dismay, ♑ could not decipher or decode what Elyon was willing to disclose.

Tiring of toiling in frustration, Azazel was preparing to part with the soft stone, to cast it down from the pinnacle. As ♑ lifted it over ♑ head to heave it, ♑ saw the reflection of the message on the gold pinnacle.

"Whattt? Would you look at that! a-z-a-z-e-l-y-o-n. My name integrated with Elyon's name. I did it." "Eureka," Azazel screamed. "I have mastered the message of Elyon. The message is in the Ark. I know what I have to do!"

♑ also saw something else for the first time, that would require another look once ♑ had solved the *'cryptogram in the crypt.'*

Azazel summoned ♑ closest confidants. "Come at once. We are going to Ikhet, into the large chamber. From henceforth, the chamber will be called the Chamber of Azazel. I am going to lie down in the Ark and your god will become your God forever."

Azazel misunderstood the message and would soon learn a lesson that ♑ would forget even faster.

Once in the chamber, Azazel began *'instructing his inferiors how to implement ♑ initiation into immortality.'*

"Lift the lid and hold it until I get inside and I tell you to put it back in place."

"With you inside?" Leviathan asked in disbelief.

"Of course with me inside, you...," Azazel hushed ♑self knowing how the demons despised what they deserved, but if ♑ angered them now, they might revolt and not let ♑ out of the Ark once the capstone was in place.

Azazel's confidence rose, seeing ♑ body was a perfect fit. It seemed that the sarcophagus was selectively sculpted for ♑.

The sound of stone scraping stone made a irritating "eeerrrcccchhh," as the lid was being closed, but Belial shouted, "stop, don't close the lid."

"Azazel tried to raise up while asking, "What is wrong? Close the ^%*$#$ lid."

Belial thought, "♑ calls us imbeciles," as ♎ sarcastically retorted, "How will we know when to let you out?"

Azazel was so anxious about getting in the crypt but had not thought about how to get out.

Speaking more out of bravado than brawn, "I want all of you to leave Ikhet. If what I expect happens, I will get out on my own."

CHAPTER TWENTY-THREE
CONVERSATIONS FROM THE CRYPT

Only Elyon and Azazel know what exactly happened in the darkness of the crypt and as expected, their versions vary.

The voice of Elyon exuded a tone of tenderness previously unheard by Azazel. "Azazel, I adjure you to be attentive to what I impart to you. I will tell you of the future; the one that is and the one that can be. I led you into this crypt; into the covering of darkness that you so covet. Your folly falsely makes you think you are here of your own devices and design, but that is not so."

Azazel laughed with a nervous hilarity that hinted ♑ hoped Elyon was in error. The *'hideous heckler'* let loose, "Muahaha, muahaha, muahaha! You, muahaha, you did what? You put me here? Muahaha," ♑ ended ♑ mockery with a satanic snicker!

"You will see Azazel. If I did not put you in the Ark, try now; try now to get out on your own."

"I will not give you the enjoyment of watching me try, letting you assume I believe anything you just said," Azazel said in disgust and distrust.

"Be that as it may. I am going to share an eternal secret with you. Something that is known only by ♍. My purpose is to reveal to you the '*recklessness of your revolt and its far reaching ramifications.*'"

"I don't know why I bother, but babble on! I have no other place to be," Azazel mocked.

"This is not babbling, it is battle braggadocio. You and I are on a collision course with consequences that you cannot possibly conceive. Here it is! A parable that will grant you the foreknowledge that you hope to gain, that is if you can grasp it."

"Once a garden, ever a garden to be,
For nothing lost is everything gained,
The Earth belongs to Me.
Once was light, twice was dark,
But dark never, forever can be,
The face of the deep sees the light,
Shall new heavens and new earth begin?
They are of old, yet nothing new to Me.
A mighty man will walk the earth
Red shall be his name,
Heavens Word, his faithful friend,
Lies are trusted by his twin,
Who shall share the blame?
The flying serpent licks the dust
The dust then stings the man.
The Ancient of Days draws near,
As the Spirit doth hover,
Overshadowing to birth,
The Son of the unspoiled mother.
A child of Himself, His own Father to be,
A mystery how this flesh is Me.
Death prolongs its terror reign,
Crowning itself Master of fear,
It as Prince and you as King.
Evil thinking to win, brought to an end,
When the soldier thrusts the spear.
Death defeated, the child prevails,
By the sound of driven nails.
Your crypt, My grave
Yours lost, mine saved
To dark chambers to take the key,

One will rise, one bend their knee.
Kingdoms come, Kingdoms fall,
You cast your sullied crown to Me.
The son of the morning, evenings last light,
Now chained forever in endless night
Inferno alight, fiery flames twice heated,
Cannot cremate evil repeated.
Good ever lives for good is ever Me."

Struggling to remember every word, Azazel forgot ♑ arrogance just long enough to slip and say, "I have no idea of the meaning what you just said to me."

"I didn't expect you too, but you will. I come to this sepulture of stone to show you the shadowy reality of death; something you have never witnessed or imagined. Here and now, I should destroy your body, leaving your spirit eternally entombed in the ❖, as an example to my next creation that will dwell on earth. Even though I know your intentions, my ambition is to reform you and return you to the condition in which I created you. When I depart from you, it will be with bereavement, not over your death, but your damnation."

"You speak using fables with foolish hopes of frightening me, but I know your words are nothing more than fabrications and falsehoods. There is no death. If so, why would you not have caused my death before now?"

"This is why you can never be God Azazel. Though you despise me, you are not destroyed. Only for the fact, I made you in goodness and perfection, yet you chose a poisonous path of evil. I am God for there is no evil in Me, but I will not tolerate you forever.[1]

A disquieting silence surrounded Azazel, as the covering of darkness did not dispel ♑ creeping concern. Several times,

1 Genesis 6:3 - There are limitations to God's long suffering Grace.

He screamed, "Elyon, ♈, speak to me." Nothing! Then ♑ called out to ♑ fellow demons. "Abaddon, Pythus, Leviathan, Belial, Beelzebub, anybody!"

Nothing! ♑ remembered that ♑ ordered them all to leave. *"I will* get out on ♑ own," ♑ bellowed attempting to convince ♑self. The one who ruled by fear was now fears captive.

Azazel exhaustingly struggled until ♑ succeeded in raising one arm barely above ♑ head, high enough to scratch and pick endlessly at ♑ granite grave. ♑ elongated claw like fingernails wore down until the skin was torn. Finally, ♑ felt the first wisp of outside air from the small hole ♑ managed to open, but there was only the sound of ♑ cries for help to be heard. No one had dared to disobey ♑ and reenter Ikhet. Over and over, Azazel called for ♑ companions, but to no avail. ♑ cries were muffled and ♑ eyes stung like fire as small chunks of stone fell on ♑ as dust choked off ♑ breathing. Azazel panicked, "Perhaps death is real after all!"

CHAPTER TWENTY-FOUR
FATAL ATTRACTION

Azazel wondered if ♑ was destined to be first to experience death. Weakened, beyond being able to bend his legs to put ♑ feet against the capstone, ♑ had no real hope of escaping on ♑ own. 'The capstone just might become ♑ headstone.' Then hope came calling. It was the unmistakable high pitched voice of Lilith, "Azazel, Azazel."

♎ was the only one brave enough to breach Azazel's order, especially considering coming alone into the bowels of Ikhet, leaving the dusky light of Sol faintly behind at the entrance. Lilith felt ♎ way along the cool stone walls of the corridors, hoping not to fall into the bottomless pit if ♎ lost ♎ way before ♎ oversized white eyes could adjust to the total blackout inside the ❖.

"Azazel, Azazel, are you in here? Call back to me if you can hear me." No reply! "Azzzaaazzzel, can you hear me?" Nothing but the empty echo of ♎ own voice!

Lilith abruptly bumped into something solid. It felt different from the flat walls. "This is not a wall, it must be the crypt," ♎ surmised as ♎ ran ♎ trembling hands over the edges of the cold granite. With a startle that almost made ♎ knobby knees buckle, ♎ grabbed hold of what turned out to be a long raw finger. "What is a finger doing coming out of hard stone," ♎ wondered.

The finger moved just as Lilith heard a muffled plea for help. ♎ pressed ♎ ear near to the hole where the finger was flailing as though calling for help.

Azazel's injured finger touched the hair of yet an unknown savior. Then, ♑ knew by the texture of the soft curly hair that it was Lilith who had come to find ♑. ♑ pulled ♑

finger back into the crypt as Lilith placed ♎ ear over the small hole that Azazel had managed to open.

“Lilith, is that you?”

“Yes, Azazel it is me. I’m sorry that I disobeyed you, but I could not stand to leave you here alone and not know what was happening.”

“Hush, say no more. You have to get me out of this crypt, but promise never to tell any other how you found me.” I can’t move, but if you can push the capstone aside just enough for me to get leverage, together, we can get me out of here.”

“I can and will do anything it takes to get you out.”

It took all the strength they possessed to free Azazel from his Tomb, but after much effort they wearily walked out of Ikhet together.

“Lilith, you must go with me up to the pinnacle of Ikhet. The pinnacle is highly polished and I saw the image of myself for the first time. I was distracted at the time, but when I saw myself, I looked just like you or even better, you look just like me. I want you to see yourself and see if you think that you look like me.”

“I have never thought about what I look like, Azazel, but if I look like you, I will be beautiful.”

“I wondered about our likeness the first time that I saw the red hair on your head. I know that the hair on my body is red, but is the hair on my head red?”

“Yes it is,” Lilith said with a smile on ♎ face.

“Come on, let’s go. I can’t wait for us to see ourselves and to see each other.”

Atop the ❖, the advent of angelic attraction was afoot, but the consequences could be catastrophic for all of creation. It was apparent that they appealed to one another, for no other reason than the fact they both were haughty and conceited, two deadly traits that always lead to a destructive fall.[1]

As they gazed in amazement, Azazel breathlessly proposed, "Lilith, I think that there are no others that look like we do."

"There are no others that compare to you or I."

"Lilith, listen carefully. I am sure that I know the reason for our resemblance. While I was captive in the crypt, Elyon spoke to me of a powerful creature who would walk the Earth and be joined by a twin. No question, the powerful creature is none other than me and you are my mate. We favor because you are my fellow."[2]

Azazel and Lilith consummated their matrimony[3] made on earth while mocking the mandate of Zevul[4].

Lilith and Azazel's attraction was a dire distraction to the demons on Earth. As jealousy became the rule, they aligned themselves according to genus and color, creating competitive classes rife with envy, alienating one another. Pythus was especially effected as ♎ felt pushed aside, inflaming jealously causing ♎ searing '*red eyes to turn green with envy.*'

Azazel was increasingly inclined to listen to Lilith instead of Pythus. ♎ green eyes were no less hot and burned right through Lilith every time ♎ saw ♎. Azazel valued the advice of Lilith, sensing ♎ was candid and spoke out of true concern for ♑. Whereas, Azazel was wary of Pythus the liar and ♎ self-centered style of speaking whatever was covertly convenient!

Azazel confided to Lilith, "I wondered how Elyon

1 Proverbs 16:18 -"Pride precedes destruction and a haughty spirit before a fall."

2 Associate, companion, counterpart

3 Association

4 Zevul is the 7th heaven. The mandate or Zevul is in Matthew 22:30 - "At the resurrection people will neither marry nor be given in marriage; they will be like the angels in heaven."

claimed to be God of all, yet ♍ could not control me. Now, I make my claim, only to find I cannot control them."

"You will control them and ♍. Remember the words of Beelzebub, when ♎ advised you to be commandingly cruel. Show them no mercy, give them no food, nothing, unless they give you blind obedience."

CHAPTER TWENTY-FIVE
SATAN'S SPHINX[1] SHRINE

A Golden Era for Azazel was underway on Earth. Great advances were achieved in the sciences as ageless secrets were decoded and deciphered. Azazel could not have been more confident of ultimate success in the quest to topple Elyon as Lord of Everything! Until!

Dudael reported to Azazel, "Our knowledge has increased dramatically, although as *'accomplished rule breakers,'* there seems to be "*'unbreakable rules by which the universe is run'*" that we cannot change. Our collective genius cannot comprehend the concept of immutable absolutes.

Leviathan updated the status of the animal kingdom, they being a major player in Azazel's plan. "Many species of the animal kingdom are experiencing exponential growth in size and display disturbing changes in their nature. For no apparent reason, others collapsed and began decomposing. It is probable that *'death'* as described by ♈ is real?"

Azazel did not react to the reports, being overwhelmed with euphoria of ♑ personal ambition.

These reports prompted Pythus to suggest a scientific

1 Many archeologist believe the Great Sphinx once was a winged monument.

probe into the makeup of the material bodies of the Demons.

♎ proposed the question, "How much like the animals are we and will we die like them?"

Lilith had ♎ own agenda, "Azazel, the Earth is entirely yours, and yet the only monument here is Ikhet which we now know is Elyon's Altar upon which you were to be sacrificed. Ikhet was intended to be your death trap and your headstone. The secrets, the codes were all intended to lure you in, just like that strange flower here in the garden lures the insects, but you found a way to overcome."

"What strange flower would that be?" Azazel quizzed.

"The one that you named Venus,[1] after the beautiful planet you lusted for until you saw the Earth."

"Aha, now I get your meaning."

"You transformed Ikhet into your own temple, wisely using your crypt to convert your servants into a devoted Royal Priesthood.[2] They trust your ingenious tale that you died, were buried in Ikhet's tomb, and then resurrected yourself, remade as the reigning holder of the Key to everything. Brilliant, simply brilliant! The simpletons allow you to bury them in your tomb, thinking they change from the devils they are transformed into a royal class of angels. Elyon will forever regret that ♍ shared ♍ so-called secret with you! ♍ gave you what you wanted without a fight."

"You are right Lilith, but be assured a fight is coming; Belial and Pythus have steadily stirred up animosity against the arrogant Elyon. Abaddon reports that my army is ready to attack. *'I will'* capture ♍ throne!

1 Venus fly trap - Dionaea muscipula, is a carnivorous plant that consumes insects.

2 The business of being a Priest who practices and preaches religious dogma.

'I will' exalt my throne above♍ throne."[1]

"Your throne, hmmm," Lilith slyly pretended as though this was ♎ first time thinking this thought.

"If I could be so bold to suggest, you should construct for yourself an earthly throne that will far outshine anything in the heavens. It must be *'terrifyingly beautiful'* to inspire those who admire you and intimidate the few that would affront you. Build something that reveals your greatness and grandeur. Make the mundane talents of the self-proclaimed *'Maker'* appear secondary to your creative abilities. Erect a *'monument to your might, a monolith to your majesty,'* then you will be totally prepared to fight, to win, to reign."

Azazel had perfect recall of Elyon's throne having served as one of its guardians.

"Elyon's throne is a tedious, tiresome place. No shape or structure. Laws everywhere written all over it. Do this, don't do that. Holy, holy, holy again and again."

"That is it. That is your answer. Build your throne to transfigure who and what you are. Think of the symbols inside Ikhet. The lion, the eagle, the ox and the perfect malakim face. This is what and who you are, so why not make this your throne."

Building a sphinx structure became top priority, as was the construction of two other ❖'s heavy on Azazel's mind. ♑ heeded Lilith's advice to build a monument of great beauty, but could not get over ♑ narcissistic need to also build something bigger than Elyon's altar.

Calling together the Generals ♑ informed, "Abaddon, the builders will require the strong backs of the soldiers."

"Builders of what?"

1 Isaiah 14: 12-13 " How art thou fallen from heaven, O Lucifer, son of the morning! how art thou cut down to the ground, which didst weaken the nations! For thou hast said in thine heart, I will ascend into heaven, I will exalt my throne above the stars of God:

The Prodigal Satan

"Abu-Hol,[1] Atyhet[2] and Prathet.[3] Father of Terror, ❖ two and ❖ three."

Abaddon felt insulted at being instructed as though a common laborer. "I had hoped to meet with you concerning a pressing matter." Abaddon had pending war on ♎ mind not personal works of pernicious gratification.

"There is nothing more important to me than this. Let this be the last objection I hear. Marshall the soldiers!"

It was a herculean task, but many of the methods used in building Ikhet had been *'reverse engineered'* by Azazel's *'satanic scientist.'* ♑ also demanded much input from Ikhet's Royal astrologers. They adopted the saying, *"As above. So below."* This mantra expressed Azazel's desire to have ♑ own heaven on Earth. The stargazers observed and mapped the alignment of the three brightest stars of Orion's heavenly belt, Mintaka, Alnilam, and Alnitak and their companion stars that form *'the great Sky River.'*[4] *'The Heavenly Artist'* had painted a perfect picture of what came to be with building of the three ❖'s along the winding banks of *'the great Niel River,'*[5] long before Azazel came into being!

Azazel informed the angelic architects of ♑ wishes, "I want my monuments to represent heaven on earth showing that I from earth will rule the heavens. By ♑ command and will, a gigantic replica of a lion carved out of limestone bedrock, sprawls two hundred and forty feet long, spanning thirty-eight

1 Abu Hol - The Great sphinx. Known to the Egyptians as "Father of Terror." Sphingo means to make a complete circle or to choke by encircling. The face of Virgo and the body of Leo, the first and last constellations, encircling or possessing the constellations.

2 Atyhet - Pyramid two standing next to the Great Pyramid.

3 Prathet - Pyramid three standing next to Pyramid two.

4 The Milky Way known as the Great Sky River.

5 Ni-el meaning God's River. Now known as the Nile River in Egypt.

feet across its powerful oxen like shoulders, reaching sixty-six feet at the crest of its malakim head, with its eagle wings spreading in landing fashion, soaring one hundred forty-four feet into the air. The limestone Lion lies gazing east, steadily staring at Orion from Elysian Fields.

Lilith was exuberant; "It is hard to believe that anything could eclipse Ikhet, but just look at Abu Hol. It is both beautiful and dreadful."

Azazel criticized, "It is beautiful, but not nearly as dreadful as I would have wished. Why is the lion not pouncing and tearing at its enemies?"

"If I might explain, I consulted with the builders and instructed them that Abu Hol should lie in a resting position. This Lion has defeated every challenger and is confident that none other will come against it. It is the temperament of the Abu Hol that makes you, the terrifying lion. Its calmness boasts of its conquest. The lion has prevailed over its enemies, earning the right to preside over every power in heaven and on Earth."

"Well" said Azazel. "You have made me feel different about the Lion. Now, I have a surprise for you. Please come inside to the secret chambers that I have built inside of the belly of the beast."

Upon entering, Lilith was agape at the artistry of the subterranean structures and the content of what was a gigantic storehouse. Azazel made sure Mammon collected and brought treasures from every corner of the planet into the sphinx for safekeeping. The interior rooms of Abu Hol were cavernous repositories containing the rarities of planet Earth.

"Azazel...Oh, Azazel. I never imagined such wondrous wealth!"

"Wait, I have one other surprise to show you."

"I don't think that anything can compare to these vaults

overflowing with precious stones that stagger my sensibilities."

"There is much more, so wait before you pass judgment. Since we are bantering over beauty versus bestiality, you have beheld the beauty. Now, let me show you my crowning achievement. *'The beast in me is the one who wins'* out!"

♑ led ♎ out of the massive chamber into a tunnel treacherously descending into the Earth.

"Where are you taking me?" Lilith asked with an air of apprehension.

"It leads into the chamber in Ikhet, where lies the gaping hole opening into the bottomless pit."

"Why would you want to take me to such a place?" ♎ fear growing!

Azazel laughed with such a ghoulish guffaw, that the walls of the tunnel seemed to tremble.

Fright triggered Lilith's flight response! Azazel had to rush to grab Lilith as ♎ inadvertently ran in retreat toward the open pit in full panic.

"Stop, stop I said," ♑ shouted while dragging Lilith down! This trip into the tunnel is not meant to harm you. *'I just wanted you to taste the terror that I will unleash on any who choose to disobey me. They will be cast into the pit without mercy. The more who know of such a place, the fewer will have to experience it.'* Be true to me Lilith and I may let you be the one to cast the imps into the pit."

Lilith had no choice but to aversely agree, suspecting if ♎ refused, this may be a test of loyalty and ♎ would be the first one pushed headlong into the pit.

"We should come up with a name for the pit. A word that everyone will learn to fear," Azazel added. "What do you suggest we should name the pit?"

The Prodigal Satan

"Without thinking, ♎ blurted out, 'Sheol.'[1] It just sounded like *'the hole.'* Let's be going now. I can't wait to start spreading the word," ♎ deceptively declared. *"You are the Tzar of Terror."*

Azazel succeeded in securing the private entrance into Elyon's Altar and competing with God for un-shareable Glory. ♑ frothed with frustration at the fact that in spite of every effort, ♑ could not complete a ❖ to compete with the size and grandeur of Ikhet. This led to the intensifying talk of war against Elyon. It was left up to Abaddon to delicately alter Azazel's ill advised militant action.

1 Hebrew לואש translated as «grave,» «pit,» or «abode of the dead.» The inhabitants of Sheol were the «shades (rephaim), entities without personality or strength.

CHAPTER TWENTY-SIX
DINOSAURS OR DEMONSAURS

Abaddon secretly met with Pythus to obtain advice on how to approach Azazel. ♎ also requested Beelzebub and Leviathan to attend, only after affirming that they agreed with ♎ strategy.

The meeting began, "We would never contemplate contesting your cunning tactics Azazel, but we sought this audience to suggest some strategic planning."

"I'm listening, but the work had better continue while we wastefully cavort[1] around," Azazel sniped.

"Lord Azazel, I don't doubt you and will always follow where ever you lead. Just, please consider that we are greatly out numbered. Myriads of misguided angels stayed in the service of Elyon and it is reported that some of our number are exhibiting signs of being *'throne-sick for Elyon.'*

They avow that Elyon never treated them like slaves. They say, *'Elyon speaks and worlds appear. You speak and work appears!'"*

Azazel swore, "*I will* personally push you all into the pit. Anyone who speaks against my actions or repeats the rants of the reprobate rebels will be in peril of punishment. You are acting like someone *'throne sick?'* If you want a throne, you will have to make your own. Back to work, all of you."

Abaddon responded in the manner of a professional soldier, "Sir, we are simply reporting. If you could reserve your reaction until I have finished speaking. Please, may I continue?"

Surprisingly Azazel subdued ♑self, but the feeling was that of dead calm before a deadly storm.

1 Play around.

"Second, we have no intelligence on what weaponry Elyon possesses. I know that we have made progress, but we are yet to succeed in developing a flaming sword that turns in every direction at one time. Also, we fear we have been infiltrated. A glowing worm we named 'Shamir'[1] has appeared on earth. We have just learned of its power. It cuts through stone as though it were mud and iron like water! These are some of the weapons the soldiers of Elyon may wield."

"What flaming sword, what Shamir?" Azazel begged almost aghast. "Why have I not been informed? Would you have me to believe that we can be defeated by a flaming sword and a glowing worm?"

Abaddon eked out ♎ words with a cautious cadence, "You not being a warrior, would not have known about this weapon. Several of us have seen it. This thing makes no noise, but it sends out searing shafts of golden tipped blue flames in every direction at once, making it impossible to evade. We have no known defense for it, and Elyon may possess other weapons just a lethal as those we have no knowledge of, just as it is with Shamir. It is rumored that Bene Elyon is able to illuminate ♍self, brighter and hotter than any of the stars."

"Enough, enough I said." If looks could kill, Abaddon would be the first dead demon! Azazel glared at Abaddon as the silence hung heavy in the room.

Abaddon, unwilling to relent, finally cut through the fog, "Lastly, what would we do if Elyon should attack first?"

"♍ attack first?" The quiver in ♑ voice sent a shiver

1 Rabbis Rashi and Maimonides wrote that Shamir was a living creature, a worm. It was argued that Shamir could not have been a mineral because it was active. Rabbi Nehemiah said the Shamir was used to engrave the names of the twelve tribes on the semiprecious stones of the Urim and Thummim. Shamir is also credited for writing on the stones of the Ten Commandments and cutting the stones for the building of the Temple of Solomon.

through ♑ suddenly fearful followers.

Leviathan whispered to Beelzebub, A god and ♑ never even considered an attack a possibility!"

It only got worse for Azazel, "♍ would never attack first. ♍ is a God of love."

Azazel's alliance eroded as Beelzebub boldly challenged, "You tell us Elyon is vicious, that ♍ attempted to kill you. Who, a God of Love? Now you say we have no reason to fear an attack from ♍. What are we to believe? You trust in the love of Elyon for our survival?"

Going on the offensive, Azazel shot back, "Where are you going with this? If you have a plan, out with it now!"

Leviathan whispered again, "I hope ♑ attacks Elyon with half the ferocity that ♑ does us."

Abaddon softened the tone, "None of us know if Elyon will attack, but surely ♍ knows our intentions and is making preparations. We should be doing the same."

"And that would be?"

"It is our consensus that we should go underground. Our cities that we have built would be much safer if they were not openly exposed."

Leviathan added, "We have good cause to believe that Elyon is already seeking our destruction. I would have already brought this to your attention, but you and Lilith have been disturbingly distracted with completing the construction of your shrines."

"Impossible, I am informed of every incident that happens on my planet. This strategy session seems to be about nothing more than you informing me of my ignorance. Belial, you took an oath to report any seditious talk to me. I hold you responsible for this slander!"

"No one should have to inform you of what almost everyone on this planet already knows."

"Knows what?"

"You Azazel, you are constantly surrounded by guards, so perhaps you have not noticed the animals, the mammals or the birds. All of them have changed. When we first arrived, we had peace with every creature that swims in the sea, crawls or walks upon the Earth and the birds that fly in the heavens. A troubling thing has happened.

Their appearances, sizes and shapes have changed. Many of them have become much larger and perhaps more powerful than we are. The Earth trembles as they walk; they make huge waves in the water, diving and surfacing as though they are restless. Some have forsaken the water, exhibiting the same abilities that I have. They stand upright as I do. I know that I am assigned to falsely proclaim that we all came from the sea, but with the mammals, it is happening."

Azazel saw where this was going and it was playing into ♑ hands. He kept silent and tamed ♑ temper to set and spring ♑ trap. "Who are these imbeciles to think I don't know something?" ♑ grunted.

Azazel's murmuring didn't deter Leviathan. *"They have become aggressive toward each other and us. Their size and speed is worrisome. Lizards are now larger than the pachyderms were, rodents run swifter than leopards and Lions with ivory fangs protruding from their jaws are bigger than horses. Some species have grown multiple sets of teeth aligned on their powerful jaws. We have watched as their bite breaks the thickest of the trees like twigs. They prey on anything smaller or weaker than themselves and their glowing yellow eyes hungrily peer at us.*[1] *Even the birds of the air are of great concern. The once lowly sparrow is as large as the albatross whose wings spread in flight darken the sky."*

1 Isaiah 56:9 -"All you beasts of the field, all you beasts in the forest, come to eat."

The Prodigal Satan

"They no longer sing soft songs, but scream from the heavens as they swoop down upon other animals, tearing at them with their talons. They soon will threaten us even if Elyon doesn't. This may be the work of Elyon, to have us devoured us from above and below!"

Before Azazel could open ♑ mouth, Abaddon proposed an alternative point that might explain the revolt of nature.

"It would seem that the Earthly creatures were at peace with us until we began using our weapons of war to practice on them for the fight with Elyon. None among us imagined the possibility of the animals morphing into the monsters they have become. At first, they befriended and favored us. We caused them to fear us, so now they choose to oppose us. It is a fight we started, because we feared Elyon. Now we should fear ♍ and the animals."

"Anyone else care to be proven wrong? Who dares to think I am not aware of everything that happens on the Earth? Let me educate you. I will never fear Elyon and neither should you. None of what you have just described is attributable to Elyon.

This is what happened. I wondered how I went from being a slave to a superior, from *a groveling grunt to a great god in my own sight*. To understand this change in me, I instituted a secret study that I named DNA. This stands for *'Demonic Not Angelic'*, and I had our smartest scientist take samples of me. I am the one who is entirely evil, making me the perfect sample. I discovered that the secret of DNA is concealed in my heavenly name Satan. I am four substances, Sytosine, Adenine[1], Thymine, Adenine, and Nuanine.[2]" Do you see S-A-T-A-N? Do your see me, the one who is the substance and core of every one of you and other living creatures? *'I am*

1 2 parts Adenine

2 The organic molecules that determines ones DNA.

Satan in every lock of my hair, layer of skin, my spittle, every part of my body is wholly and wonderfully wicked.'

It was the demons turn to mumble, "What on Earth is ♑ talking about?"

"I can tell by the blank look on your faces, you are not on the same level with me. There is only one Satan!"

No one dared to jeer or cheer. They were blank but eager to hear more.

"You erroneously thought I wasn't aware that some among you yearn to return to Elyon. Anyone feeling such an emotion is nothing like me. My consuming desire is to defeat Elyon and eradicate ♍ memory forever, even if I must destroy everything to accomplish it."

Curiosity changed to a concern!

"I took captive several complainers, suspecting that their DNA would be different from mine. I was right. Enough of this lesson that you will never learn. Besides, anyone caught complaining will be checked. If found to have goodness in their DNA, they will be sentenced to Sheol."

Leviathan inquired, "What if anything does this have to do with the danger we face from the animals."

"The animals are only as dangerous as I make them."

"You make them? What kind of talk is that?"

"Stand down and shut up Leviathan, I'm trying to tell you. Pythus suggested what I have already accomplished, when ♎ called for a study of our bodies. When will you and the others ever acknowledge that you cannot get ahead of me?"

"We didn't know it was a contest."

"It isn't. A contest requires contestants, but I have none who can compete with me. My grand experiment was to see what would happen if I put my DNA in the animals. My nature combined with their strength, size and speed is a weapon to be reckoned with. They will hate Elyon. They must, a part of me is now in them."

"You may have created something that you can't control," Belial daringly hinted.

"You fool, I would not be so stupid. If I have power to create new species of animals, would I not also know how to destroy them. We discovered an animal whose saliva is identical to that of the Seraphim. We named this animal *'snake'* and after putting my DNA into the snake, it grew fangs and began biting other animals. They quickly died. Died, you heard right! Dead! I now control the deadliest secret of Elyon. It is called *'venom.'* Not even Elyon has ever destroyed anything. If ♍ controlled death, surely I would be dead. Look at the carcasses strewn across the face of this planet. What a beautiful sight to behold. If this does not challenge Elyon to come down here and fight, then *I will* ascend into the heavens and fight with ♍."

All of *demon-dom* was smitten with awe!

"You have watched monstrous beasts collapse and decompose. You have seen the swiftest fall and rot. This is death, even Elyon's dreaded death and I am its Master. I can easily rid us of the *'demonsarus'* by allowing them to devour one another, but I prefer to conqueror than kill them. *'I will'* trap, tame and train them. The monsters you fear most are what we will use to fight. Imagine, Elyon's creation, ♍ creatures under my command; recreated by me to war against ♍. My DNA in them and them fighting Elyon is the same as me fighting Elyon."

"But how can we be sure that they will fight Elyon and not turn and fight against us?"

"Azazel lifted up from the Earth and landed precisely posturing ♑self on the head of Abu Hol. Innumerable demons rushed to see what would happen next. Eyes of all colors pierced the shade of Earth's dusky light as ♑ pointed at the massive head of Abu Hol.

"I fashioned this gigantic Lion that crouches alongside Ikhet. Whose image is it that sits as the head of the great beast? Mine," Azazel answered ♑self emphatically. "The Lion is formed in my likeness. Come near and see for yourselves. My name is engraved on the forehead and the claws of the beast. These encompassing marks reveal my rightful rulership over the animal kingdom. It is a sign to you and to any other kingdom on Earth or in heaven, whether animal or angel; I rule everywhere and reign supreme over everything!"

Abaddon was first to fall to ♎ trembling knees in fear. All of demon-dom did likewise, as a sign of their remorse for challenging Azazel.

'An unsettled sobriety settled over the Kingdom of Chaos controlled by the King of Crisis!' The advancements made by Azazel and ♑ hordes could be considered admirable achievements for any civilization if it were not for the fact that each endeavor pointed to one ending. The overthrow of Elyon and usurping ownership of every possession of ♈ was paramount in Azazel's planning.

The Prodigal Satan

A SECRET WEAPON - RUBBLE FROM RAHAB
CHAPTER TWENTY-SEVEN

Psalms 89:9-14 -"Thou rulest the raging of the sea (on Earth): when the waves thereof arise, thou stillest them. Thou hast broken Rahab in pieces (in the heavens), as one that is slain; thou hast scattered thine enemies (Satan and his fallen angels) with thy strong arm. The heavens are thine, the earth also is thine: as for the world and the fullness thereof, thou hast founded them...Justice and judgment are the habitation of thy throne."

♈ being the Captain of the Host assembled His war counsel with Michael and Gabriel.

"I have called you together, as an apocalyptic attack from Azazel and ♑ fallen followers is imminent. As you know, 'I Am' a just God and any war that I prosecute must be based in righteousness and justice. The following violations are my indictments against ♑. First, I charge Satan with slanderous lies. Lying is especially offensive to me, in that it imitates my creative ability. *Lying is a product of deceit with its roots in imaginary nothingness presented as reality, creating delusional illusions.* 'Creating something from nothing is a power belonging solely to me.'

Second, Satan is guilty of rebelling against my authority, which has adversely affected many of My angels. ♑ continuously blasphemes everything that is Holy.

Third, ♑ is convicted of covetousness, commandeering control of the Earth and ravaging it of every precious treasure just for the thrill of taking from ♍. The *Earth is no longer pristine; its environment is poisoned, the pure waters are polluted and the once peaceful animals are abused and turned into terrible beasts.*

The Prodigal Satan

Michael mused, "♈, we are not surprised at the report, but it is alarming to hear it succinctly stated. This kindles my anger like fire. Let me go to Earth and I will smite Azazel for ♑ rebellious ways."

"I feel the heat of your heartfelt passion, but it would mean the end of Earth to fight Azazel there. ♑ is determined, to ♑ detriment, to destroy my throne and to replace it with ♑ own. ♑ openly stated that ♑ will ascend into the heavens and exalt ♑ throne above that of mine. Azazel has never believed that I know ♑ thoughts. We will use ♑ plans against ♑ to affect ♑ defeat."

Michael earnestly inquired, "Lord, what must we do to wage this war with you?"

"You and Gabriel will have a vital role. This war will be fought in ways that Satan never imagined. ♑ foolishly would employ tactics such as using the animals of Earth to attack us and has exerted much energy to train them to do exactly that. This could only happen if we went down among them.

By my grace, I have never revoked the demons permission to return here, to *'their first abode,'* but animals were made for Earth life only. Oh, the things that Azazel does not know! ♑ infected them with ♑ genes which warped their docile demeanor and altered their shapes and sizes, changing them into demonsarus! Sadly, I have determined to destroy the animals along with Azazel. As soon as Azazel lifts up from the earth to begin the conflict, I will cause a cataclysmic event to commence on Earth. A wind named 'Euroclydon'[1] will whip up across the seas driving deep waters[2] across the land enveloping the face of the Earth. Every living thing remaining

1 Euroclydon is a cyclonic tempestuous northeast wind which blows in the Mediterranean. Mentioned in Acts 27:15 as a Nor'easter!

2 Job 26:11-14 - "The pillars of the heavens tremble, awe-struck at his (the Lord's) threats. By his power, he has whipped up the Sea (on Earth)," Jerusalem Bible.

on the Earth will perish. Cities and civilization will wash away and be no more.[1] Only My Altar and certain reminders of Satan's rebellion will remain as a record of the Earth and My plan for it."

"Lord, we know there must not be an alternative or you would avail yourself of it."

"What will become of Satan and to where will ♑ flee?"

"As most anyone in peril would do. ♑ will attempt to return to ♑ ancient abode."

"Rahab?"

"Yes, Rahab."

"Is it at all in your plan to allow ♑ to return?"

"No. There will be no place for ♑ to flee. I will use Rahab as a weapon against ♑ and ♑ army. I will destroy Rahab, breaking it in pieces."[2]

"Lord, Rahab is one of the greatest of all the stones; how is it that it will be destroyed?"

"This will be your duty Gabriel. I will provide you a mighty war trumpet to sound and the noise of its blast will rival that of creation. I will add my breath to your blast."[3]

"You are to sound it seven times. Each blast will destroy a portion of Rahab, starting with its oceans which will vaporize, then it's crust will dry and crumble. Its mantles will melt and its core cremate. Azazel and ♑ warriors led by Abaddon will hear it, thinking it to be the sound of their battle trumpet.

1 Jeremiah 4:23-26 -"I looked at the earth, and it was formless and empty; and at the heavens, and their light was gone. I looked at the mountains, and they were quaking; all the hills were swaying. I looked, and there were no people; every bird in the sky had flown away. I looked, and the fruitful land was a desert; all its towns lay in ruins before the Lord, before his fierce anger."

2 Job 26:12-13 "By his skill, he has crushed Rahab (Satan's planet). His hand has pierced the fleeing serpent." Jerusalem Bible.

3 Job 26:13 "His breath has made the heavens luminous" (the blackness of space lit up by the impact explosion) Jerusalem Bible.

This will rouse them beyond being rational or reasonable. They will launch an all out attack against my Throne. We will wait until they are passing through Maon. Then the seventh sounding of the trumpet aided by my voice will shatter Rahab into innumerable pieces of rock. I, accompanied by Michael will go down to meet Azazel in Machon as the fragments of Rahab's rock mercilessly rain down on the rebels, but not one pebble will come near us."

"How can this be?"

"Even the stones hear my voice. I could command stones to become bread and it would be so."

"Be it unto us to win this battle with you."

"When Rahab explodes, the heavens will illuminate[1] with the effulgence of My Glory. I tell you these things now so great fear does not come upon you. You have never seen my glory used, as it shall be. The destruction from this battle will be devastating. l will crush Rahab and use its shattering pieces to beat back Azazel and ♑ army into full retreat down to the Earth where flood waters will overflow and drown them all."

"What will happen to the surrounding planets?"

"The planetary bodies will be pummeled with burning pieces of Rahab hurdling through the heavens. They will be seared, scorched and scarred as a somber reminder of the *destruction* in store for the disobedient.

Gabriel and Michael trembled as their understanding of *'destruction'* came about. "Lord, does this mean that Azazel and ♑ demons will no longer exist?"

"I made them eternal spirit beings, not eternal bodies. Everything that I do is designed to maintain perfection in my presence. I will destroy their bodies with the prospect of penitence that could purge their spirits of all impurities if they will return in repentance to Me. *'I will not cause ruin without*

1 Job 26:13 -The explosion of Rahab lit up the heavens.

the prospect of restoration in mind.'"

Michael asked, "Gabriel will sound the trumpet as you shout, but what is my assignment?"

"You Michael are going into battle with a power second only to Mine. Come down with me so not one unrepentant demon escapes My judgment."

Michael was full of wrath against the wanton demons and wondered, "Will ♈ accept fallen angels back into ♑ Kingdom?"

"I will curse the water and the air. Nothing that swims in the water, crawls upon the face of the Earth or flies in the atmosphere will be allowed to live. All of Earth has been infected with *'Demon genes'* and must be destroyed. You and your legions are to walk the Earth and capture anything that survives the aerial assault I have ordained for Azazel and ♑ followers. I am sending Uriel with you. ♎ eyes will run everywhere like lightning searching over, under and through everything on the face of the Earth, so that nothing escapes the destruction."

"To do your will O' God is my pleasure!"

"When you have made an end of executing the demoniacs that will not repent, take the captives into my altar and cast them into the pit with no bottom. I will place a door over the opening to the pit and you are to chain it closed and secure the key."

With ♎ fiery eyes ablaze with resolve, Michael pledged, "I lift my right hand to you that none but You will ever possess the key to the door concealing the pit."

"Gabriel, you will descend to Maon to stand firm with the flaming sword, protecting the sanctity of our sanctuary. No evil spirit will ever be allowed to ascend beyond Machon unless they are bidden by Me to facilitate My will."

The Prodigal Satan

Michael and Gabriel cast furtive looks at one another, not comprehending what ♈ just said. Neither of them chose to ask or question ♈, but they pondered, "For what reason would ♈ ever allow Satan or ♑ kind access to the highest regions ever again?"

Michael bowed ♎ head and lowered ♎ voice to a most humble tone, "Master you speak of repentance and the return of the rebellious. How can these things be?"

"Ramiel will fly through the third heaven proclaiming My Mercy for those who will turn from Satan, renounce the serpent and accept My salvation. I know those who are truly remorseful and the others who are impostors. Raguel will be on hand to administer My Justice."

"Aha, my Lord, I understand that You know all things. We will welcome those You redeem and war with those You refuse."

"Raphael will take up residence in the third heaven once it is secured. ♎ will cleanse the atmosphere of the *'putrid spirits that have polluted it with their presence.'* Saraquel will remain in ♎ place around the Throne and will coordinate all angelic activity from there."

The battle lines were drawn and victory assured for ♈. Azazel never imagined what indignation was to be unleashed upon ♑. *The compliance with commands in the Kingdom of light starkly contrasted to the disruption and disorder in the Kingdom of darkness!*

Bene Elyon took one last look.

The Crimson Cord was still red!

CHAPTER TWENTY-EIGHT
PRIDE ON PARADE

Proverbs 16:18 -"Pride goes before destruction, and a haughty spirit before a fall."

Azazel summoned ♑ war council, "We must do something to entice ♈ to come to Earth or else, we will fight ♈ in the heavens."

Belial replied, "We know how much ♈ loves this stone...

Azazel perceived what Belial was about to say but despised taking counsel from g council. "Yes, I know and my plan is to create such havoc here, ♈ cannot resist coming to rescue the Earth."

Abaddon added, "Once ♈ is defeated here, the myth of Elyon will be manifested and our march into Zevul will be unimpeded. ♍ throne will be easily taken and ♍ servants will become our slaves."

Mammon was thinking of material gain, "Once we have possession of the heavens, we can harvest the metals from every stone, both heavy and light, using them to gain wealth and make weapons of warfare. [1]

Every planet will be our quarry, ours to plunder its treasures as we have here on Earth."

Abaddon could read boredom on Azazel's countenance and surmised, "One would think that this kind of talk would please Azazel." Mammon had yet to learn, *'it's impossible to appease inherent evil.' 'Evil is an appetite never satisfied and*

1 Ezekiel 28:4-5 - "With thy wisdom and with thine understanding thou hast gotten thee riches, and hast gotten gold and silver into thy treasures: by thy great wisdom and by thy traffic hast thou increased thy riches, and thine heart is lifted up because of thy riches:"

a thirst never slaked.'

"You see the massive sinkhole from whence the trees of knowledge and life were uprooted, but yet do not grasp the greatest treasure accessible to me."

Abaddon shook ♎ gnarly head in disbelief. "What could be greater than having your enemies as your slaves, your arch rival eradicated, and the treasures of the universe all yours? As I have your attention, I have thought that we should capture and bring ♈ here to ♈ beloved Earth, parade ♈ to ♈ pyramid altar and sacrifice ♈ there. Whatever is left of ♈ can be cast into the pit with no bottom. There are many vile demons that you put there because of their wavering affection toward you. Those held captive there will surely blame ♈ for their plight. If any part of ♈ is left alive, it will be pleasurable to know ♈ is being tortured and tormented."

Azazel irately screamed, "It's the trees you imps. To possess the Tree of Knowledge of both good and evil and of the Tree of Life is the ultimate. Why has not one of you ever thought of taking back our trees?"

The usual pall of silence gripped the goblins upon realizing *'Azazel is not merely some angry angel.'* They chanted. "Azazel indeed is Satan ... Azazel is Satan."

Pythus could not resist, "Lord Azazel, your anger arouses us to action. Your hatred haunts us to do evil. Your lies are what we listen to and love. Your rebellion will rule us forever."

Azazel calmed in ♑ bipolar way, "We are all the wiser having learned the lessons of Ikhet, but it appears no one but me believes there is more to be gained. *'The more is in the trees.'* I partook of but one bite of the tree of knowledge and look how advanced I am compared to any of you. *'I will'* take both trees for myself! Why do none of you ever think about the tree of life? ♈ told me that I would never die, because I tasted the Tree of Life, but you have no such assurance. *'You must fight for the tree.'* If you care to live, fight for the tree."

'The Master Motivator' had them riled and ranting, *'The tree, the tree, the tree belongs to me! Knowledge good, knowledge evil. The tree, the tree, the tree belongs to me!'*

As the chant continued, Dudael saw what was happening and hurried to get to the message to the others. Dudael imagined, "If Azazel gains control of the trees, ♑ will have complete control over us."

Perhaps the others were thinking the same. Abaddon whispered to Leviathan and Beelzebub, "This fight just took on new meaning. For me, it won't be about enthroning Azazel or enjoining ♑ battle, it is a struggle for our survival, a fight to the finish!"

Beelzebub seditiously suggested, "If Azazel were to lose," but stopped short when ♎ noticed Azazel shooting suspicious looks in their direction.

Leviathan finished, "We could take over."

"Abaddon, Beelzebub, Leviathan, I need to meet with you three privately," Azazel said with some austerity.

The three looked inquisitively at one another. Abaddon turned ♎ back to Azazel to quietly pose the question, "Did ♑ overhear us?" Abaddon nervously jumped when unexpectedly ♎ felt a tap on ♎ shoulder and spun around to see Azazel staring at ♎ straight in ♎ face.

Azazel sarcastically suggested, "Jumpy about the fight are you?"

"No, no not at all," Abaddon quickly recovered.

"I hope not. You as commander must be the calmest of all. This is why I have chosen you to lead the charge. Beelzebub and Leviathan will be with you. I will be in the rear so that I can see the entire battlefield to direct you and make sure that none of our troops defect."

The Prodigal Satan

Once the three were alone, Abaddon blurted out, "Azazel must have heard us. ♑ is setting us up."

Beelzebub admitted, "We may be as much of a threat to ♑ as ♈. It may be time for a revolt of a different kind!"

'For such is the Kingdom of Satan!'

CHAPTER TWENTY-NINE
PISCES IN PIECES

Jeremiah 4:26 – "I looked, and, behold, the fruitful place was a wilderness; and all its cities were broken down before the face of Jehovah, before his glowing anger. For so Jehovah has said, The whole land shall be a desolation; yet I will not make a full end."

Jeremiah 4:29 – "For this shall the earth mourn, and the heavens above be black; because I have spoken it, I have purposed it, and will not repent, neither will I turn back from it..."

Revelation 12:7 - "And there was war in heaven: Michael and his angels fought against the dragon; and the dragon fought and his angels fought back."

Mark 13:25 - "The stars will be seen falling from the firmament, and the forces which are in the heavens will be disordered and disturbed."

The higher heights of heaven were abuzz with action as Elyon gave the command for the advance on Azazel to begin.

"For this shall the earth mourn, and the heavens above be black; because I have spoken it, I have purposed it, and will not repent, neither will I turn back from it." [1]

The first act of war came suddenly! Satan's preference for darkness over light was granted as Elyon shut down the power supply to the heavens. *Without as much as a flicker, the pulsars pulses flat lined into a faded facade of what had been the stars.* In one blink of Azazel's slanted eyelids, *'the soft grey*

1 Jeremiah 4:28.

shade of Earth dissipated into mournful, mutilated shades.'[1] Devoid of light, the heavenly bodies wandered aimlessly, wobbling from their orbits becoming easy prey for what are snake like holes in the universe that angels use as *'travel tunnels.'* The *'Black Holes'*[2] *'imploded'* in size, transforming into inescapable dark swirling vortexes, swallowing distant stars and planets into their inescapable densities, spewing them out into *'a place of protection'* [3] *known only to Elyon,* far out of the reach of Satan's greedy grasp. Strangely, every animal went silent as a *'harbinger'* [4] of *'the Holy-caust'* about to happen. *The birds, whales and porpoises stopped singing, the mammals ceased croaking their guttural sounds. No canine howls, wild animal growls. Even the viols of Azazel's pipes refused to emit music in concert with ♑ movement.*

The surf made no sound as it ceased curling ashore and the sea became like glass. The laboring demons dropped their implements and the clamor of the builder's tools constructing Azazel's kingdom no longer rang out. Satan's slaves stared into the midnight of utter darkness with a maddening feeling of frightful dread of something unprecedented and unknown. *The sound of silence was deafening. All was quiet but far from calm!*

The Malakim stationed at Ikhet's shaft that opened toward the constellation Leo noticed it first. ♎ shrieked, "Something just happened. It appears that the heavens are on fire."

What ♎ saw was the steam of at least a Septillion or more gallons of sea water vaporized at once from the ocean

1 "Mournful mutilated shades" - Dante's Inferno Chapter 29.

2 A black hole is a region of space time from which gravity prevents anything, including light, from escaping.

3 Vilon - The 7th Heaven beyond the view of men or demons."

4 Something that precedes or foreshadows a future event .

floor of the watery planet Rahab.

"Do you feel it?" Leviathan questioned.

Leviathan may have felt it first since ♎ was the heaviest creature on Earth.

Beelzebub affirmed, "Yes. Yes I do feel it. I feel as light as a bird. I am having a hard time keeping my feet on the ground." ♎ statement had much meaning as the eagles, vultures, ravens, doves, owls, nesting birds and waterfowl lifted up from the earth, ascended into the heavens unable to return to their perch or nest, even as they furiously flapped against the change in the atmosphere. The rivers and streams sought out different courses and channels, running one way, then another causing the fish of every kind, crocodiles, alligators, water serpents, jellyfish, whales, manatees and hippopotamus to boil to the surface. Even creatures of the deep known only to Elyon and never seen by any other; not even by the eye of Leviathan, rose from the depths of Earth's ocean to parade off into the vastness of space.

The change in the Earth's orbit and its wobble hurled every demon and creature into the heavens as gravity gave way to Elyon's command. Nothing remained stationery, secured or fixed on Earth, with the exception of Ikhet and the sphinx, ♈'s altar and Satan's stelae.[1] Huge boulders bulged from the surface of the earth; trees without deep roots wrested free from the firm grip of their soil and every structure built by Azazel's laboring demons began ripping apart, ascending into the heavens. The Earth trembled and quaked at the sudden and severe changes!

Azazel didn't know what was happening but was quick to exploit the event.

1 Stelae were also used to publish laws and decrees, to record a ruler's exploits and honors, to mark sacred territories or mortgaged properties, as territorial markers or to commemorate military victories.

The Prodigal Satan

"Abaddon, this is it. The fight is on. Order the army to attack."

"Order you say? The entire earth is in disarray and chaotic disorder and you scream orders? Look at us Azazel, we are being flung through the heavens like trash in the wind and you say 'order!' The soldiers cannot lay hold of their weapons or retrieve their armor. They reach for their swords only to find a dead sparrow in their hand. They try to take hold of their shields but lose grip. Their weapons are covered with the slippery slime of snakes and fish, yet you command me to order."

Pythus heard Abaddon's retort and added, "I fear that we all are being ordered alright, but the orders are not coming from you Azazel. I suspect that we are being summoned to a slaughter by *'One Superior' to...*"

Azazel not letting Pythus finish ♎ sentence, screamed, "You filthy liar, I should never have trusted you."

Beelzebub gasped as ♎ *'tumbled and twisted in resistance against the nothingness of no resistance.'*[1] I am smothering in this refuse heap of bodies, rubbish and rubble.

Azazel just started to curse Beelzebub, but ♎ sentence was shortened by the piercing sound of a war trumpet. "Phaaaaa-paaaa-rahhhhh!!!" Its blast was accompanied by the shout of Gabriel, "The Son Is Coming!"[2]

1 Weightlessness???

2 Translated from Book 5, Chapter 6 of Josephus' Jewish Wars Greek text by William Whiston, reads as follows: "...Now, the stones that were cast [by the Roman catapults during the siege of Jerusalem] were of the weight of a talent, and were carried two furlongs and farther. ...As for the Jews, they at first watched the coming of the stone, for it was of a white color, and could therefore not only be perceived by the great noise it made, but could be seen also before it came by its brightness; accordingly the watchmen that sat upon the towers gave them [the Jewish rebels] notice when the engine was let go, and the stone came from it, and cried aloud in their own country language, "THE SON COMETH:"

The Prodigal Satan

Then there was a second blast, "Phaaaaa-paaaa-rahhhhh!" Then a third, fourth, fifth, sixth and lastly...! As the trumpet sounded the seventh time, the Earth reeled just as the *'Sound'* of the exploding planet Rahab caught up with its companion, *'Light.'* The roar pierced the heavens as it reached Azazel's pointed ears.

"The flash nearly blinded me and now I cannot hear," Azazel complained, but no one else could hear ♑.

Abaddon lamented to ♎self, "I am not prepared to go into battle not knowing what it is that I fight against. No one heard ♎ either.

It was a *'moot point to the mute warriors,'* who were now uncontrollably winging their way upward to a war that many of them didn't want. Earth's gravity lost its grip!

Abaddon struggled to gain control, "We have trained for this. Prepare for battle," ♎ shouted repeatedly as ♎ rapidly ascended heavenward. "Stay calm, collect your weapons."

The atmosphere was cluttered with the dead and dying bodies of Earth's animals who soon suffocated in the vacuum of Machon. The aerobatic[1] armor, arrows, swords and other weaponry of the demons, went wildly wayward, slashing, piercing and punishing dying animals and the demons alike. Together, they jostled in the air until the lower heavens resembled a *macabre mosaic.*

Azazel's vision cleared just enough for ♑ to search the sky for Lilith. ♑ exerted every ounce of energy to stay *'shielded'* behind the others for ♑ safety, but also supposing Lilith would look for ♑ there. It was a bloody place to be!

Satan screamed to Abaddon, "♈ must have known of my plan to use the animals against ♈. Some God of Love, who slaughters ♍ own creatures."

Suddenly, *a pealing plea from the powerful voice of*

1 Spectacular or dangerous maneuvers done in the air.

The Prodigal Satan

Ramiel proclaimed, "Mercy to those who accept ♈ invitation to return as Sons of God into His service. Repent and receive forgiveness and favor with ♈." *A roar of repentance rolled throughout the heavens as many demons renounced their allegiance to Azazel.*

"Forgive us ♈, forgive us for serving Satan. Forgive us," they screamed over and over. Their pleadings were answered in blood as their cries attracted the attention of Ramiel who made sure none were neglected.

"No, no; it is a trick of your enemy! Satan mistook the *crimson cruor*[1] to be poison, but it was a *'potion of pardon.'*

"What is this ghastly colored stuff covering many of my warriors and slaves?"

Dudael choked, "It is blood! The blood of the slaughtered animals."

Pythus wondered, "Why is it only the blood of sheep, oxen and doves that runs like a crimson river. Yet the carnivores, reptiles and demonsarus, shed no blood."

Miraculously, the warm red blood of the slain, shedding animals accumulated in the much colder upper atmosphere of the third heaven, but did not coagulate. Every demon, whether lowly Malakim or soaring Seraphim's; whosoever called out for mercy was instantly immersed[2] in the blood.

"Satan watched in wonder as those baptized in animal blood passed through the seemingly impregnable bloody barrier and beyond, advancing past Machon?"

"The spin doctor Pythus explained, ♈ is likely taking the pathetic peons to the fire burning in Leo to punish them. ♈ knows they are weak unlike us."

"A fire near unto Leo? That is where Rahab is located. Would the &*%^#$ dare to destroy my home?" It was too late

1 Blood

2 Baptized

for cursing and daring. *'Rahab was now nothing more than trillions of pieces of smoldering stones of all shapes and sizes having been smitten by the 'Fist*[1] *of Elyon.'*

Again Dudael reasoned. "The fire in the upper heavens is undeniable. Rahab is unlikely to have been burned, but none of that explains why we cannot break through the bloody barrier of Maon."

"So you say Dudael. Azazel, send the doubters away and let we, the warriors do what we do. The blood of animals stopping the greatest army in the universe?" "Never," Commander Abaddon bragged!

Beelzebub regained enough equilibrium to explore exactly what was happening. Peering in the direction of Rakia, ♎ became the sentinel sounding the alarm.

"The heavens are falling," ♎ bellowed! "Retreat, retreat, retreat!"

Hearing Beelzebub bellow in full-blown panic caused mass pandemonium. Retreat trumpets blared everywhere but the demons were suspended in space with no way to escape.

Leviathan grunted, "I'm breaking out of this bloody trap." ♎ made a furious charge at the invisible barrier, but to no avail. Azazel cowardly desired to be last of the warriors in the line and was working hard on making ♑ rapid retreat reality.

"Back to Earth, we will fight from there," ♑ screamed. Some of the demons hopelessly mocked at the foolishness of Azazel as ♑ helplessly assaulted the lower level of Machon, with the same result as Leviathan.

"We can barely move in the condition we find ourselves and the fool Azazel shouts commands as though g is in control!"

God's incoming *'guided missiles'* lit up Rakia, then

1 Anthropomorphic expression. The fist, hand, arm, eye, etc. of God is not literal, but God accommodating His self to human thought or comprehension.

Shechakim, Zevul and Maon. As the burning rubble of Rahab penetrated Machon, every eye saw the glaring white stone *'Wormwood,'*[1] as it noiselessly seared its way toward the earth dragging one third of the crushed pieces of Rahab in tow as it charged through the cosmos. The whiteness accentuated by its blazing tail resembled another Sol. The first to feel the impact of the *meteoroids*[2] and *asteroids*[3] created by the crushing of Rahab was Rahab's nearest neighbors. *'The two planets Mars and Jupiter were pummeled and pocked by the megalithic bombardment they suffered as collateral damage to Rahab's destruction.'* Earth would be next, but for now, Azazel, Lilith, Abaddon, Pythus, Beelzebub, Dudael and every other demon were the targets of these *planetary projectiles. Each piece whether bit or bolder was named, ordained, orbited with a targeted object as its objective.*

"Looking up and feeling helpless as ♎ watched the burning sky barrel down on them, Abaddon could only think, "Your shields. Soldiers, place your shields above your heads and prepare for impact." Again, it was a silly order born of desperation with no hope of implementation.

"Our shields," some demons frantically screeched in disgust. "Our swords and shields are scattered like startled birds across the heavens. Abaddon asks us to build a fortress out of nothing. ♎ is blind, stupid or both!"

By Elyon's design, the bloody barrier of Machon did not prevent pelting shards and residue of Rahab from penetrating, and preparing a gaping hole. The massive chasm engulfed every demon not covered in animal blood.

1 Revelation 8:10 - "And the third angel sounded, and there fell a great star from heaven, burning as it were a lamp..." Revelation 8:11 - "The name of the star is Wormwood."

2 A small body moving in the solar system before it enters Earth's atmosphere.

3 A small body moving in the solar system before it enters Earth's atmosphere.

The Prodigal Satan

Screams of utter terror erupted as the pummeled demons plummeted toward the Earth. *A scene never imagined became heaven's horror show as multiplied millions of evil ones grabbed and tore at one another in hope of shielding their selves from the sharp stones incessantly pelting them.* They hopelessly plunged headlong in the vapor trail of wormwood as it targeted *Earth.*[1]

Azazel cried out, "Cover me, you imbeciles. I am your only hope. Cover me I said. If I die, we all die."

For once, the truth came from ♑ lie stained lips. The line was crossed and every demon had a *date with death. If Satan should survive, then Elyon is a liar and a fraud!*

1 Jeremiah 50:22-25 - "A sound of battle is in the land, and of great destruction. How is the hammer (Satan) of the whole earth cut asunder and broken! I have laid a snare for you, and you are also taken, O Babylon (Kingdom of Satan), and you were not aware: You are found, and also caught, because you have warred against the LORD. The LORD has opened his armory, and hath brought forth the weapons of his indignation: (flaming swords and a shattered planet) for this is the work of the Lord GOD of hosts..." Author's Translation

CHAPTER THIRTY
WOUNDED AND WASTED WORLDS

Genesis 1:2 -"Now the earth BECAME formless and empty." NIV

Job 26:5,6,11-13 - "The departed spirits and their inhabitants tremble Under the waters. Naked is Sheol before Him And Abaddon has no covering..." "He obscures the face of the full moon, And spreads His cloud over it ..." "The pillars of heaven tremble, and are amazed at His rebuke. He quieted the sea with His power, And by His understanding He shattered Rahab. By His breath the heavens are cleared. His hand has pierced the fleeing serpent." NASB

The collision of Earth and Wormwood was so violent that the Earth shuddered and shook until every part of it, down to its molten core, was moved. Trillions of tons of rock and debris were hurled into the atmosphere. An equivalent amount or more of Rahab's rocks came tearing into the Earth, searing and scarring its surface. Every element was enveloped in embers as Wormwood enkindled them, leaving Earth without an atmosphere to protect it. The incoming assault of meteors met no resistance. The erratic misbehavior of the planets eradicated gravitational force from Earth causing its foundations to break apart and its strata's to shift, shaking and quaking Elyon's crown jewel.

Molten lava gushed from beneath the Earth's surface, bursting open like putrid boils, blistering towering mountains into existence. Massive tsunamis raced from one end of the Earth to another entirely inundating the planet.

'Seconds after Wormwood's impact a runaway shard of Rahab struck Satan, piercing ♑ badly bruised body,

slamming ♑ into the Earth like a strike of lightning.'[1] Azazel prophesied, even as ♑ was perishing, *"The first to die, I shall be the King of death!"* These were the last words of Satan spoken while in ♑ primeval body.

Abaddon's shields failed to fend off the onslaught of fiery stones as every rebelling demon was being beaten down into the rising water covering the Earth. The noise of multitudes of pinioned creatures screeching, shrieking, and struggling to stay out of the swelling sea, was terrifying.

Then came Michael accompanied by a heavenly host of warring angels, each armed with laser like flaming swords. As the angels furiously whirled their weapons above their heads, rays of bluish green light radiated in every direction targeting and pinpointing the demons who had not already drowned. The strange light from the angel's swords was excruciating for the evil dark ones to endure. They were helplessly paralyzed by the phosphorescent swords, rendering them unable to swim or thrash about, being overcome in the swelling waters of death.

What looked to be the ultimate destruction of Earth and the surrounding heavens was in reality the beginning of Elyon's rearranging the heavenly bodies and the Earth for their survival. Not only was Elyon positioning every planet, star and heavenly body for Earth's good, the message of the luminaries would be forever changed. Satan could no longer read or rightfully interpret the *'gospel of the stars'* or the firmament.

A loud voice from Heaven prophesied of what to us would be our next, but was already accomplished in the Eternal 'now' of Elyon.

"Awake, awake, put on your strength, O' arm of the LORD, awake as you did long ago, in days gone by. Is it

1 Luke 10:18 - "I beheld Satan fall from heaven like lightning!" See Cover artwork

not You who hacked Rahab in pieces and ran the dragon through? Was it not You who dried up the sea, the waters of the great abyss. The LORD of Hosts is Your name. The cleft of the sea and its waves roared, that You might fix (nata, fasten or set) the heavens in place and form (yacad, settle, establish the foundations of) the earth." [1] The outcome of a battle being fought for control of the Earth was old news in heaven. What are *'days gone by'* to Angels, demons or humans is nothing to a *'timeless God.'*

What seemed to be the ultimate destruction of Earth and the surrounding heavens was Elyon rewriting the Heavens. Elyon reshaped and rearranged the cosmos and all creation, for re-creation! *'The benevolent blacksmith'* of heaven *'hammered'* out the new heavens and new Earth.[2] God recycled the solar system so Satan no longer can decipher the eternal truths displayed on the vast canvas of outer space. ♍ spelled out ♍ message using shining starry spheres as the alphabet of ♍ pictorial language. The luminaries are situated to conceal God's truths from and confuse demonic despots. Nor is ♑ allowed to investigate or desecrate the Altar of Elyon at will. ♑ Sphinx memorial is allowed to remain lying on the scorching desert sand of what once was a beautiful garden. The massive man, ox, lion of Egypt is eroded with watermarks high up its sides as a testimony to the terrible judgment of a Righteous God against rebellion! The eagle like wings of the Sphinx were broken off and destroyed by Elyon. Satan is evicted from the heights of the upper heavens, with no pass or access to the Throne that ♑ disdained and desecrated.

Elyon summoned an ancient, yet to be illuminated

1 Isaiah 51:9-16 Authors Translation.

2 Isaiah 42:5 - "Yahweh, who created (bara) the heavens and spread them out, who hammered into shape the earth." Jerusalem Bible

dark star[1] named Sol[2] and situated it in perfect position to provide light and warmth to Earth whenever 'time comes'[3] to turn the lights back on. Seeing the end of the war was at hand, Gabriel announced to the angelic population, *"God you divided the sea by your strength: You broke the heads of the dragons in the waters. The day will be yours, the night also is for you: You have prepared[4] the moon[5] and the sun. You have set all the borders of the earth: thou hast made summer and winter."*[6]

Wormwood's size and speed careening into planet Earth created a crater covering one-third of its surface. The waters of Earth flushed into the chasm created by the exploding stone, eroding great canyons in what previously was soft seabed. Elyon designed watery graves to accomplish the destruction and decomposition of the defaced bodies of the demons. Untold tons of sand, silt and soil churned and covered the grotesque corpses of the cursed demons and demonsarus deep inside the bowels of a world turned upside

1 A dark star is a type of star that may have existed early in the universe before conventional stars were able to form. The stars are composed mostly of normal matter, like modern stars, but a high concentration of neutralino dark matter within them generates heat via annihilation reactions between the dark-matter particles. Wikipedia

2 Earth's star named Sun.

3 Genesis 1:4 "And God said, "Let there be light," and there was light. God saw that the light was good, and he separated the light from the darkness."

4 Psalms 74:16 "The day is yours, and yours also the night; you established (kuwn) the sun and moon." Hebrew word 'kuwn' meaning, stood perpendicular, heaped up. Which likely means the moon was formed by material 'heaped up' when the Earth was radically judged."

5 Psalms 74:16 "The day is yours, and yours also the night; you established the sun and moon (Maor)." Hebrew word 'maor' meaning, light giver, the moon.

6 Psalms 74:17 - "It was you who set all the boundaries of the earth you made both summer and winter." Accomplished by tilting Earth's axis with the asteroid's impact.

down.

Again a voice from Heaven spoke, *"I looked on the earth, and beheld it laid Prodigal and void; and to the heavens, and they had no light. I looked on the mountains, and, behold, they quaked. And all the hills were shaken. I beheld and lo, there was no being; and all the cover of the skies had fled."* [1]

The scene in Heaven made for a telling contrast to that of Earth. Bene Elyon entered Maon, greeted with astounding adoration by every living creature. *'The loudest shouts of praise came from the redeemed angels now restored into the Kingdom of Elyon!'*

They needed little encouragement from Gabriel, who led out, *"Praise him, all his angels; praise him, all his heavenly hosts."*[2]

It was not a coronation for Bene Elyon for ♈ already was King, rather a confirmation of the unyielding loyalty of a Host that would never again be hostile to its Heavenly ruler! It looked much like this when the Angels saw ♈! *"Who is this coming from Edom, from Bozrah, with his garments stained crimson?*[3] *Who is this, robed in splendor, striding forward in the greatness of his strength?* Bene Elyon shouted back, *"It is I, proclaiming victory, mighty to save."*[4]

The crimson colored cord of the "Firstborn" was elegantly draped about the waist of its rightful Righteous owner!

Elyon ceased from warring and the Earth lay wounded, wasted and waiting! [5]

1 Jeremiah 4:23-25 - Author's translation.

2 Psalms 148:2

3 Isaiah 63:1

4 Isaiah 63:1

5 I looked at the earth, and it was formless and empty; and at the heavens, and their light was gone.

ABOUT THE AUTHOR

Pastor, Educator, Evangelist, Mentor and Author.

Louis presently serves as Pastor of The Encouragers Church of St. Peters, Missouri. This is Pastor Green's second Novel. The first, "The Crimson Cord" has gained wide acceptance in the Christian community as well a secular circles. The Crimson Cord has been classified as a 'Historical Novel" due to the years of research Louis put into the religion of Baal, which is a major part of the plot of the book. Likewise, The Prodigal Satan is very much a product of the author's first hand knowledge of Egypt and especially of the Great Pyramid, he having climbed to its apex of 455 feet some years ago. This combined with Egyptian archeological experience and 48 year career in Biblical studies has highly qualified Louis to compose this Novel.

Made in the USA
Columbia, SC
15 November 2024

46504550R00100